ARCHIE AND NERO WERE
THE STAR SUSPECTS IN
A LAVISH PRODUCTION OF MURDER!

"The bodies were piling up and the D.A. was getting sore. He suspected Wolfe and I were withholding evidence—which we were—so he grabbed me as a material witness. He was threatening to haul Wolfe in too when the phone rang.

"It was Wolfe. If there's one thing that annoys him more than cyanide poisoning it's having me arrested. Unless I was immediately released, Wolfe declared, he was going to tell the newspapers he had solved the case—with no help from the police.

"It was a spectacular bluff. I walked out knowing that within twenty-four hours Wolfe and I had to catch the killer, or I'd be going back—in leg irons."

A NERO WOLFE NOVEL

AND BE A VILLAIN

BY REX STOUT

Meet it is I set it down,
That one may smile, and smile, and be a villain . . .
HAMLET, Act 1

AND BE A VILLAIN

*A Bantam Book / published by arrangement with
Viking Penguin Inc.*

PRINTING HISTORY

*Viking edition published September 1948
Dollar Mystery Guild Selection published November 1948*
2nd printing ...... December 1948
3rd printing .... May 1949
Book League of America edition published February 1949
2nd printing. .... January 1949
3rd printing .... January 1949
*Bantam edition / October 1950
New Bantam edition / January 1961*

3rd printing .... May 1968	6th printing . September 1969
4th printing .... June 1968	7th printing .. February 1970
5th printing . September 1968	8th printing .. December 1975
9th printing .... October 1979	

1

For THE third time I went over the final additions and subtractions on the first page of Form 1040, to make good and sure. Then I swiveled my chair to face Nero Wolfe, who was seated behind his desk to the right of mine reading a book of poems by a guy named Van Doren, Mark Van Doren. So I thought I might as well use a poetry word.

"It's bleak," I said.

There was no sign that he heard.

"Bleak," I repeated. "If it means what I think it does. Bleak!"

His eyes didn't lift from the page, but he murmured, "What's bleak?"

"Figures." I leaned to slide the Form 1040 across the waxed grain of his desk. "This is March thirteenth. Four thousand three hundred and twelve dollars and sixty-eight cents, in addition to the four quarterly installments already paid. Then we have to send in 1040-ES for 1948, and a check for ten thousand bucks goes with it." I clasped my fingers at the back of my head and asked grimly, "Bleak or not?"

He asked what the bank balance was and I told him. "Of course," I conceded, "that will take care of the two wallops from our rich uncle just mentioned, also a loaf of bread and a sliver of shad roe, but weeks pass and bills arrive, not to be so crude as to speak of paying Fritz and Theodore and me."

Wolfe had put down the poetry and was scowling at the Form 1040, pretending he could add. I raised my voice:

"But you own this house and furniture, except the chair and other items in my room which I bought myself, and you're the boss and you know best. Sure. That electric company bird would have been good for at least a grand over and above expenses on his forgery problem, but you couldn't be bothered. Mrs. What's-her-name would have paid twice that, plenty, for the lowdown on that so-called musician, but you were too busy reading. That lawyer by the name of Clifford was in a bad hole and had to buy help, but he had dandruff. That actress and her gentleman protector—"

"Archie. Shut up."

"Yes, sir. Also what do you do? You come down from your beautiful orchids day before yesterday and breeze in here and tell me merrily to draw another man-size check for that World Government outfit. When I meekly mention that the science of bookkeeping has two main branches, first addition and second subtraction—"

"Leave the room!"

I snarled in his direction, swiveled back to my desk position, got the typewriter in place, inserted paper with carbon, and started to tap out, from my work sheet, Schedule G for line 6 of Schedule C. Time passed and I went on with the job, now and then darting a glance to the right to see if he had had the brass to resume on the book. He hadn't. He was leaning back in his chair, which was big enough for two but not two of him, motionless, with his eyes closed. The tempest was raging. I had a private grin and went on with my work. Somewhat later, when I was finishing Schedule F for line 16 of Schedule C, a growl came from him:

"Archie."

"Yes, sir." I swiveled.

"A man condemning the income tax because of the annoyance it gives him or the expense it puts him to is merely a dog baring its teeth, and he forfeits the privileges of civilized discourse. But it is permissible to criticize it on other and impersonal grounds. A government, like an individual, spends money for any or all of three reasons: because it needs to, because it wants to, or simply because it has it to spend. The last is much the shabbiest. It is arguable, if not manifest, that a substantial proportion of this great spring flood of billions pouring into the Treasury will in effect get spent for that last shabby reason."

"Yeah. So we deduct something? How do I word it?"

Wolfe half opened his eyes. "You are sure of your figures?"

"Only too sure."

"Did you cheat much?"

"Average. Nothing indecent."

"I have to pay the amounts you named?"

"Either that or forfeit some privileges."

"Very well." Wolfe sighed clear down, sat a minute, and straightened in his chair. "Confound it. There was a time when a thousand dinars a year was ample for me. Get Mr. Richards of the Federal Broadcasting Company."

I frowned at him, trying to guess; then, because I knew he was using up a lot of energy sitting up straight, I gave up,

2

found the number in the book, dialed, and, by using Wolfe's name, got through to Richards three minutes under par for a vice-president. Wolfe took his phone, exchanged greetings, and went on:

"In my office two years ago, Mr. Richards, when you handed me a check, you said that you felt you were still in my debt—in spite of the size of the check. So I'm presuming to ask a favor of you. I want some confidential information. What amount of money is involved, weekly let us say, in the radio program of Miss Madeline Fraser?"

"Oh." There was a pause. Richards's voice had been friendly and even warm. Now it backed off a little: "How did you get connected with that?"

"I'm not connected with it, not in any way. But I would appreciate the information—confidentially. Is it too much for me?"

"It's an extremely unfortunate situation, for Miss Fraser, for the network, for the sponsors—everyone concerned. You wouldn't care to tell me why you're interested?"

"I'd rather not." Wolfe was brusque. "I'm sorry I bothered you—"

"You're not bothering me, or if you are you're welcome. The information you want isn't published, but everyone in radio knows it. Everyone in radio knows everything. Exactly what do you want?"

"The total sum involved."

"Well . . . let's see . . . counting air time, it's on nearly two hundred stations . . . production, talent, scripts, everything . . . roughly, thirty thousand dollars a week."

"Nonsense," Wolfe said curtly.

"Why nonsense?"

"It's monstrous. That's over a million and a half a year."

"No, around a million and a quarter, on account of the summer vacation."

"Even so. I suppose Miss Fraser gets a material segment of it?"

"Quite material. Everyone knows that too. Her take is around five thousand a week, but the way she splits it with her manager, Miss Koppel, is one thing everyone doesn't know—at least I don't." Richards's voice had warmed up again. "You know, Mr. Wolfe, if you felt like doing me a little favor right back you could tell me confidentially what you want with this."

But all he got from Wolfe was thanks, and he was gentleman enough to take them without insisting on the return

3

favor. After Wolfe had pushed the phone away he remarked to me:

"Good heavens. Twelve hundred thousand dollars!"

I, feeling better because it was obvious what he was up to, grinned at him. "Yes, sir. You would go over big on the air. You could read poetry. By the way, if you want to hear her earn her segment, she's on every Tuesday and Friday morning from eleven to twelve. You'd get pointers. Was that your idea?"

"No." He was gruff. "My idea is to land a job I know how to do. Take your notebook. These instructions will be a little complicated on account of the contingencies to be provided for."

I got my notebook from a drawer.

2

AFTER three tries that Saturday at the listed Manhattan number of Madeline Fraser, with "don't answer" as the only result, I finally resorted to Lon Cohen of the *Gazette* and he dug it out for me that both Miss Fraser and her manager, Miss Deborah Koppel, were week-ending up in Connecticut.

As a citizen in good standing—anyway pretty good—my tendency was to wish the New York Police Department good luck in its contacts with crime, but I frankly hoped that Inspector Cramer and his homicide scientists wouldn't get Scotch tape on the Orchard case before we had a chance to inspect the contents. Judging from the newspaper accounts I had read, it didn't seem likely that Cramer was getting set to toot a trumpet, but you can never tell how much is being held back, so I was all for driving to Connecticut and horning in on the week end, but Wolfe vetoed it and told me to wait until Monday.

By noon Sunday he had finished the book of poems and was drawing pictures of horses on sheets from his memo pad, testing a theory he had run across somewhere that you can analyze a man's character from the way he draws a horse. I had completed Forms 1040 and 1040-ES and, with checks enclosed, they had been mailed. After lunch I hung around the kitchen a while, listening to Wolfe and Fritz Brenner, the chef and household jewel, arguing whether horse mackerel is as good as Mediterranean tunny fish for *vitello tonnato*—which, as prepared by Fritz, is the finest thing on earth to do with tender young veal. When the argument began to bore me because there was no Mediterranean tunny fish to be had anyhow, I went up to the top floor, to the plant rooms that had been built on the roof, and spent a couple of hours with Theodore Horstmann on the germination records. Then, remembering that on account of a date with a lady I wouldn't have the evening for it, I went down three flights to the office, took the newspapers for five days to my desk, and read everything they had on the Orchard case.

When I had finished I wasn't a bit worried that Monday morning's paper would confront me with a headline that the cops had wrapped it up.

3

THE BEST I was able to get on the phone was an appointment for 3:00 P.M., so at that hour Monday afternoon I entered the lobby of an apartment house in the upper Seventies between Madison and Park. It was the palace type, with rugs bought by the acre, but with the effect somewhat spoiled, as it so often is, by a rubber runner on the main traffic lane merely because the sidewalk was wet with rain. That's no way to run a palace. If a rug gets a damp dirty footprint, what the hell, toss it out and roll out another one, that's the palace spirit.

I told the distinguished-looking hallman that my name was Archie Goodwin and I was bound for Miss Fraser's apartment. He got a slip of paper from his pocket, consulted it, nodded, and inquired:

"And? Anything else?"

I stretched my neck to bring my mouth within a foot of his ear, and whispered to him:

"Oatmeal."

He nodded again, signaled with his hand to the elevator man, who was standing outside the door of his car fifteen paces away, and said in a cultivated voice, "Ten B."

"Tell me," I requested, "about this password gag, is it just since the murder trouble or has it always been so?"

He gave me an icy look and turned his back. I told the back:

"That costs you a nickel. I fully intended to give you a nickel."

With the elevator man I decided not to speak at all. He agreed. Out at the tenth floor, I found myself in a box no bigger than the elevator, another palace trick, with a door to the left marked 10A and one to the right marked 10B. The elevator man stayed there until I had pushed the button on the latter, and the door had opened and I had entered.

The woman who had let me in, who might easily have been a female wrestling champion twenty years back, said, "Excuse me, I'm in a hurry," and beat it on a trot. I called after her, "My name's Goodwin!" but got no reaction.

I advanced four steps, took off my hat and coat and dropped them on a chair, and made a survey. I was in a big square sort of a hall, with doors off to the left and in the wall ahead. To the right, instead of a wall and doors, it just spread out into an enormous living room which contained at least twenty different kinds of furniture. My eye was professionally trained to take in anything from a complicated street scene to a speck on a man's collar, and really get it, but for the job of accurately describing that room I would have charged double. Two of the outstanding items were a chrome-and-red-leather bar with stools to match and a massive old black walnut table with carved legs and edges. That should convey the tone of the place.

There was nobody in sight, but I could hear voices. I advanced to pick out a chair to sit on, saw none that I thought much of, and settled on a divan ten feet long and four feet wide, covered with green burlap. A near-by chair had pink embroidered silk. I was trying to decide what kind of a horse the person who furnished that room would draw, when company entered the square hall sector from one of the doors in the far wall—two men, one young and handsome, the other middle-aged and bald, both loaded down with photographic equipment, including a tripod.

"She's showing her age," the young man said.

"Age hell," the bald man retorted, "she's had a murder, hasn't she? Have you ever had a murder?" He caught sight of me and asked his companion, "Who's that?"

"I don't know, never saw him before." The young man was trying to open the entrance door without dropping anything. He succeeded, and they passed through, and the door closed behind them.

In a minute another of the doors in the square hall opened and the female wrestler appeared. She came in my direction, but, reaching me, trotted on by, made for a door near a corner off to the left, opened it, and was gone.

I was beginning to feel neglected.

Ten minutes more and I decided to take the offensive. I was on my feet and had taken a couple of steps when there was another entrance, again from an inside door at the far side of the square hall, and I halted. The newcomer headed for me, not at a jerky trot but with a smooth easy flow, saying as she approached:

"Mr. Goodwin?"

I admitted it.

"I'm Deborah Koppel." She offered her hand. "We never really catch up with ourselves around here."

She had already given me two surprises. At first glance I had thought her eyes were small and insignificant, but when she faced me and talked I saw they were quite large, very dark, and certainly shrewd. Also, because she was short and fat, I had expected the hand I took to be pudgy and moist, but it was firm and strong though small. Her complexion was dark and her dress was black. Everything about her was either black or dark, except the gray, almost white by comparison, showing in her night-black hair.

"You told Miss Fraser on the phone," she was saying in her high thin voice, "that you have a suggestion for her from Mr. Nero Wolfe."

"That's right."

"She's very busy. Of course she always is. I'm her manager. Would you care to tell me about it?"

"I'd tell you anything," I declared. "But I work for Mr. Wolfe. His instructions are to tell Miss Fraser, but now, having met you, I'd like to tell her *and* you."

She smiled. The smile was friendly, but it made her eyes look even shrewder. "Very good ad libbing," she said approvingly. "I wouldn't want you to disobey your instructions. Will it take long?"

"That depends. Somewhere between five minutes and five hours."

"By no means five hours. Please be as brief as you can. Come this way."

She turned and started for the square hall and I followed. We went through a door, crossed a room that had a piano, a bed, and an electric refrigerator in it, which left it anybody's guess how to name it, and on through another door into a corner room big enough to have six windows, three on one side and three on another. Every object in it, and it was anything but empty, was either pale yellow or pale blue. The wood, both the trim and the furniture, was painted blue, but other things—rugs, upholstery, curtains, bed coverlet—were divided indiscriminately between the two colors. Among the few exceptions were the bindings of the books on the shelves and the clothes of the blond young man who was seated on a chair. The woman lying on the bed kept to the scheme, with her lemon-colored house gown and her light blue slippers.

The blond young man rose and came to meet us, changing expression on the way. My first glimpse of his face had shown me a gloomy frown, but now his eyes beamed with welcome and his mouth was arranged into a smile that would have done a brush salesman proud. I suppose he did it from force of habit, but it was uncalled for because I was the one who was going to sell something.

"Mr. Goodwin," Deborah Koppel said. "Mr. Meadows."

"Bill Meadows. Just make it Bill, everyone does." His handshake was out of stock but he had the muscle for it. "So you're Archie Goodwin? This is a real pleasure! The next best thing to meeting the great Nero Wolfe himself!"

A rich contralto voice broke in:

"This is my rest period, Mr. Goodwin, and they won't let me get up. I'm not even supposed to talk, but when the time comes that I don't talk—!"

I stepped across to the bed, and as I took the hand Madeline Fraser offered she smiled. It wasn't a shrewd smile like Deborah Koppel's or a synthetic one like Bill Meadows's, but just a smile from her to me. Her gray-green eyes didn't give the impression that she was measuring me, though she probably was, and I sure was measuring her. She was slender but not skinny and she looked quite long, stretched out on the bed. With no makeup on it at all it was quite possible to look at her face without having to resist an impulse to look somewhere else, which was darned good for a woman certainly close to forty and probably a little past it, especially since I personally can see no point in spending eyesight on females over thirty.

"You know," she said, "I have often been tempted—bring chairs up, Bill—to ask Nero Wolfe to be a guest on my program."

She said it like a trained broadcaster, breaking it up so it

8

would sound natural but arranging the inflections so that listeners of any mental age whatever would get it.

"I'm afraid," I told her with a grin, "that he wouldn't accept unless you ran wires to his office and broadcast from there. He never leaves home on business, and rarely for anything at all." I lowered myself onto one of the chairs Bill had brought up, and he and Deborah Koppel took the other two.

Madeline Fraser nodded. "Yes, I know." She had turned on her side to see me without twisting her neck, and the hip curving up under the thin yellow gown made her seem not quite so slender. "Is that just a publicity trick or does he really like it?"

"I guess both. He's very lazy, and he's scared to death of moving objects, especially things on wheels."

"Wonderful! Tell me all about him."

"Some other time, Lina," Deborah Koppel put in. "Mr. Goodwin has a suggestion for you, and you have a broadcast tomorrow and haven't even looked at the script."

"My God, is it Monday already?"

"Monday and half past three," Deborah said patiently.

The radio prima donna's torso propped up to perpendicular as if someone had given her a violent jerk. "What's the suggestion?" she demanded, and flopped back again.

"What made him think of it," I said, "was something that happened to him Saturday. This great nation took him for a ride. Two rides. The Rides of March."

"Income tax? Me too. But what—"

"That's good!" Bill Meadows exclaimed. "Where did you get it? Has it been on the air?"

"Not that I know of. I created it yesterday morning while I was brushing my teeth."

"We'll give you ten bucks for it—no, wait a minute." He turned to Deborah. "What percentage of our audience ever heard of the Ides of March?"

"One-half of one," she said as if she were quoting a published statistic. "Cut."

"You can have it for a dollar," I offered generously. "Mr. Wolfe's suggestion will cost you a lot more. Like everyone in the upper brackets, he's broke." My eyes were meeting the gray-green gaze of Madeline Fraser. "He suggests that you hire him to investigate the murder of Cyril Orchard."

"Oh, Lord," Bill Meadows protested, and brought his hands up to press the heels of his palms against his eyes. Deborah

9

Koppel looked at him, then at Madeline Fraser, and took in air for a deep sigh. Miss Fraser shook her head, and suddenly looked older and more in need of makeup.

"We have decided," she said, "that the only thing we can do about that is forget it as soon as possible. We have ruled it out of conversation."

"That would be fine and sensible," I conceded, "if you could make everyone, including the cops and the papers, obey the rule. But aside from the difficulty of shutting people up about any old kind of a murder, even a dull one, it was simply too good a show. Maybe you don't realize how good. Your program has an eight million audience, twice a week. Your guests were a horse-race tipster and a professor of mathematics from a big university. And smack in the middle of the program one of them makes terrible noises right into the microphone, and keels over, and pretty soon he's dead, and he got the poison right there on the broadcast, in the product of one of your sponsors."

I darted glances at the other two and then back to the woman on the bed. "I knew I might meet any one of a dozen attitudes here, but I sure didn't expect this one. If you don't know, you ought to, that one like that doesn't get ruled out of conversation, not only not in a week, but not in twenty years —not when the question is still open who provided the poison. Twenty years from now people would still be arguing about who was it, Madeline Fraser or Deborah Koppel or Bill Meadows or Nathan Traub or F. O. Savarese or Elinor Vance or Nancylee Shepherd or Tully Strong—"

The door came open and the female wrestler entered and announced in a hasty breath:

"Mr. Strong is here."

"Send him in, Cora," Miss Fraser told her.

I suppose I would have been struck by the contrast between Tully Strong and his name if I hadn't known what to expect from his pictures in the papers. He looked like them in the obvious points—the rimless spectacles, the thin lips, the long neck, the hair brushed flat—but somehow in the flesh he didn't look as dumb and vacant as the pictures. I got that much noted while he was being greeted, by the time he turned to me for the introduction.

"Mr. Strong," Deborah Koppel told me, "is the secretary of our Sponsors' Council."

"Yes, I know."

"Mr. Goodwin," she told him, "has called with a suggestion from Nero Wolfe. Mr. Wolfe is a private detective."

"Yes, I know." Tully Strong smiled at me. With lips as thin as his it is often difficult to tell whether it's a smile or a grimace, but I would have called it a smile, especially when he added, "We are both famous, aren't we? Of course you are accustomed to the glare of the spotlight, but it is quite new to me." He sat down. "What does Mr. Wolfe suggest?"

"He thinks Miss Fraser ought to hire him to look into the murder of Cyril Orchard."

"Damn Cyril Orchard." Yes, it had been a smile, for now it was a grimace, and it was quite different. "Damn him to hell!"

"That's pretty tough," Bill Meadows objected, "since he may be there right now."

Strong ignored him to ask me, "Aren't the police giving us enough trouble without deliberately hiring someone to give us more?"

"Sure they are," I agreed, "but that's a shortsighted view of it. The person who is really giving you trouble is the one who put the poison in the Hi-Spot. As I was explaining when you came, the trouble will go on for years unless and until he gets tapped on the shoulder. Of course the police may get him, but they've had it for six days now and you know how far they've got. The one that stops the trouble will be the one that puts it where it belongs. Do you know that Mr. Wolfe is smart or shall I go into that?"

"I had hoped," Deborah Koppel put in, "that Mr. Wolfe's suggestion would be something concrete. That he had a . . . an idea."

"Nope." I made it definite. "His only idea is to get paid twenty thousand dollars for ending the trouble."

Bill Meadows let out a whistle. Deborah Koppel smiled at me. Tully Strong protested indignantly:

"Twenty thousand!"

"Not from me," said Madeline Fraser, fully as definite as I had been. "I really must get to work on my broadcast, Mr. Goodwin."

"Now wait a minute." I concentrated on her. "That's only one of my points, getting the trouble over, and not the best one. Look at it this way. You and your program have had a lot of publicity out of this, haven't you?"

She groaned. "Publicity, my God! The man calls it publicity!"

"So it is," I maintained, "but out of the wrong barrel. And it's going to keep coming, still out of the wrong barrel, whether you like it or not. Again tomorrow every paper in

11

town will have your name in a front-page headline. You can't help that, but you can decide what the headline will say. As it stands now you know darned well what it will say. What if, instead of that, it announces that you have engaged Nero Wolfe to investigate the murder of the guest on your program because of your passionate desire to see justice done? The piece would explain the terms of the arrangement; you are to pay the expenses of the investigation—unpadded, we don't pad expenses—and that's all you are to pay unless Mr. Wolfe gets the murderer with evidence to convict. If he comes through you pay him a fee of twenty thousand dollars. Would that get the headline or not? What kind of publicity would it be, still out of the wrong barrel? What percentage of your audience and the general public would it persuade, not only that you and yours are innocent, but that you are a hero to sacrifice a fortune for the sake of justice? Ninety-nine and one-half per cent. Very few of them would stop to consider that both the expenses and the fee will be deductible on your income tax and, in your bracket, the actual cost to you would be around four thousand dollars, no more. In the public mind you would no longer be one of the suspects in a sensational murder case, being hunted—you would be a champion of the people, *hunting* a murderer."

I spread out my hands. "And you would get all that, Miss Fraser, even if Mr. Wolfe had the worst flop of his career and all it cost you was expenses. Nobody could say you hadn't tried. It's a big bargain for you. Mr. Wolfe almost never takes a case on a contingent basis, but when he needs money he breaks rules, especially his own."

Madeline Fraser had closed her eyes. Now she opened them again, and again her smile was just from her to me. "The way you tell it," she said, "it certainly is a bargain.—What do you think, Debby?"

"I think I like it," Miss Koppel said cautiously. "It would have to be discussed with the network and agencies and sponsors."

"Mr. Goodwin."

I turned my head. "Yes, Mr. Strong?"

Tully Strong had removed his spectacles and was blinking at me. "You understand that I am only the secretary of the Council of the sponsors of Miss Fraser's program, and I have no real authority. But I know how they feel about this, two of them in particular, and of course it is my duty to report this conversation to them without delay, and I can tell you off the record that it is extremely probable they would prefer to accept Mr. Wolfe's offer on their own account. For the impression on the public I think they would consider it desirable that Mr. Wolfe should be paid by them—on the terms stated by you. Still off the record, I believe this would apply especially to the makers of Hi-Spot. That's the bottled drink the poison was put into."

"Yeah, I know it is." I looked around at the four faces. "I'm sort of in a hole. I hoped to close a deal with Miss Fraser before I left here, but Miss Koppel says it has to be discussed with others, and now Mr. Strong thinks the sponsors may want to take it over. The trouble is the delay. It's already six days old, and Mr. Wolfe should get to work at once. Tonight if possible, tomorrow at the latest."

"Not to mention," Bill Meadows said, smiling at me, "that he has to get ahead of the cops and keep ahead if he wants to collect. It seems to me—Hello, Elinor!" He left his chair in a hurry. "How about it?"

The girl who had entered without announcement tossed him a nod and a word and came toward the bed with rapid steps. I say girl because, although according to the newspapers Elinor Vance already had under her belt a Smith diploma, a play written and nearly produced, and two years as script writer for the Madeline Fraser program, she looked as if she had at least eight years to go to reach my deadline. As she crossed to us the thought struck me how few there are who still look attractive even when they're obviously way behind on sleep and played out to the point where they're about ready to drop.

"I'm sorry to be so late, Lina," she said all in a breath, "but they kept me down there all day, at the District Attorney's office . . . I couldn't make them understand . . . they're terrible, those men are . . ."

She stopped, and her body started to shake all over.

"Goddam it," Bill Meadows said savagely. "I'll get you a drink."

"I'm already getting it, Bill," Tully Strong called from a side of the room.

"Flop here on the bed," Miss Fraser said, getting her feet out of the way.

"It's nearly five o'clock." It was Miss Koppel's quiet determined voice. "We're going to start to work right now or I'll phone and cancel tomorrow's broadcast."

I stood up, facing Madeline Fraser, looking down at her. "What about it? Can this be settled tonight?"

"I don't see how." She was stroking Elinor Vance's shoulder. "With a broadcast to get up, and people to consult . . ."

"Then tomorrow morning?"

Tully Strong, approaching with the drink for Elinor Vance, handed it to her and then spoke to me:

"I'll phone you tomorrow, before noon if possible."

"Good for you," I told him, and beat it.

4

WITHOUT at all intending to, I certainly had turned it into a seller's market.

The only development that Monday evening came not from the prospective customers, but from Inspector Cramer of Homicide, in the form of a phone call just before Fritz summoned Wolfe and me to dinner. It was nothing shattering. Cramer merely asked to speak to Wolfe, and asked him:

"Who's paying you on the Orchard case?"

"No one," Wolfe said curtly.

"No? Then Goodwin drives your car up to Seventy-eighth Street just to test the tires?"

"It's my car, Mr. Cramer, and I help to pay for the streets."

It ended in a stalemate, and Wolfe and I moved across the hall to the dining room, to eat fried shrimps and Cape Cod clam cakes With those items Fritz serves a sour sauce thick with mushrooms which is habit-forming.

Tuesday morning the fun began, with the first phone call arriving before Wolfe got down to the office. Of course that didn't mean sunup, since his morning hours upstairs with Theodore and the orchids are always and forever from nine to eleven. First was Richards of the Federal Broadcasting Company. It is left to my discretion whether to buzz the plant rooms or not, and this seemed to call for it, since Richards had done us a favor the day before. When I got him through to Wolfe it appeared that what he wanted was to introduce another FBC vice-president, a Mr. Beech. What Mr. Beech wanted was to ask why the hell Wolfe hadn't gone straight to the FBC with his suggestion about murder, though he didn't put it that way. He was very affable. The impression I got, listening in as instructed, was that the network had had its tongue hanging out for years, waiting and hoping for an excuse to hand Wolfe a hunk of dough. Wolfe was polite to him but didn't actually apologize.

Second was Tully Strong, the secretary of the Sponsors' Council, and I conversed with him myself. He strongly hoped that we had made no commitment with Miss Fraser or the network or anyone else because, as he had surmised, some of the sponsors were interested and one of them was excited. That one, he told me off the record, was the Hi-Spot Company, which, since the poison had been served to the victim in a bottle of Hi-Spot, The Drink You Dream Of, would fight for its exclusive right to take Wolfe up. I told him I would refer it to Wolfe without prejudice when he came down at eleven o'clock.

Third was Lon Cohen of the *Gazette*, who said talk was going around and would I kindly remember that on Saturday he had moved heaven and earth for me to find out where Madeline Fraser was, and how did it stand right now? I bandied words with him.

Fourth was a man with a smooth, low-pitched voice who gave his name as Nathan Traub, which was one of the names that had been made familiar to the public by the newspaper stories. I knew, naturally, that he was an executive of the advertising agency which handled the accounts of three of the Fraser sponsors, since I had read the papers. He seemed to be a little confused as to just what he wanted, but I gathered that the agency felt that it would be immoral for Wolfe to close any deal with anyone concerned without getting an okay from the agency. Having met a few agency men in my travels, I thought it was nice of them not to extend it to cover any deal with anyone about anything. I told him he might hear from us later.

Fifth was Deborah Koppel. She said that Miss Fraser was going on the air in twenty minutes and had been too busy to talk with the people who must be consulted, but that she was favorably inclined toward Wolfe's suggestion and would give us something definite before the day ended.

So by eleven o'clock, when two things happened simultaneously—Wolfe's entering the office and my turning on the radio and tuning it to the FBC station, WPIT—it was unquestionably a seller's market.

Throughout Madeline Fraser's broadcast Wolfe leaned back in his chair behind his desk with his eyes shut. I sat until I got restless and then moved around, with the only interruptions a couple of phone calls. Bill Meadows was of course on with her, as her stooge and feeder, since that was his job, and the guests for the day were an eminent fashion designer and one of the Ten Best-Dressed Women. The guests were eminently lousy and Bill was nothing to write home about, but there was no getting away from it that Fraser was good. Her voice was good, her timing was good, and even when she was talking about White Birch Soap you would almost as soon leave it on as turn it off. I had listened in on her the preceding Friday for the first time, no doubt along with several million others, and again I had to hand it to her for sitting on a very hot spot without a twitch or a wriggle.

It must have been sizzling hot when she got to that place in the program where bottles of Hi-Spot were opened and poured into glasses—drinks for the two guests and Bill Meadows and herself. I don't know who had made the decision the preceding Friday, her first broadcast after Orchard's death, to leave that in, but if she did she had her nerve. Whoever had made the decision, it had been up to her to carry the ball, and she had sailed right through as if no bottle of Hi-Spot had ever been known even to make anyone belch, let alone utter a shrill cry, claw at the air, have convulsions, and die. Today she delivered again. There was no false note, no quiver, no slack or speedup, nothing; and I must admit that Bill handled it well too. The guests were terrible, but that was the style to which they had accustomed us.

When it was over and I had turned the radio off Wolfe muttered:

"That's an extremely dangerous woman."

I would have been more impressed if I hadn't known so well his conviction that all women alive are either extremely dangerous or extremely dumb. So I merely said:

"If you mean she's damn clever I agree. She's awful good."

He shook his head. "I mean the purpose she allows her cleverness to serve. That unspeakable prepared biscuit flour! Fritz and I have tried it. Those things she calls Sweeties! Pfui! And that salad dressing abomination—we have tried that too, in an emergency. What they do to stomachs heaven knows, but that woman is ingeniously and deliberately conspiring in the corruption of millions of palates. She should be stopped!"

"Okay, stop her. Pin a murder on her. Though I must admit, having seen—"

The phone rang. It was Mr. Beech of FBC, wanting to know if we had made any promises to Tully Strong or to anyone else connected with any of the sponsors, and if so whom and what? When he had been attended to I remarked to Wolfe:

"I think it would be a good plan to line up Saul and Orrie and Fred—"

The phone rang. It was a man who gave his name as Owen, saying he was in charge of public relations for the Hi-Spot Company, asking if he could come down to West Thirty-fifth Street on the run for a talk with Nero Wolfe. I stalled him with some difficulty and hung up. Wolfe observed, removing the cap from a bottle of beer which Fritz had brought:

"I must first find out what's going on. If it appears that the police are as stumped as—"

The phone rang. It was Nathan Traub, the agency man, wanting to know everything.

Up till lunch, and during lunch, and after lunch, the phone rang. They were having one hell of a time trying to get it decided how they would split the honor. Wolfe began to get really irritated and so did I. His afternoon hours upstairs with the plants are from four to six, and it was just as he was leaving the office, headed for his elevator in the hall, that word came that a big conference was on in Beech's office in the FBC building on Forty-sixth Street.

At that, when they once got together apparently they dealt the cards and played the hands without any more horsing around, for it was still short of five o'clock when the phone rang once more. I answered it and heard a voice I had heard before that day:

"Mr. Goodwin? This is Deborah Koppel. It's all arranged."

"Good. How?"

"I'm talking on behalf of Miss Fraser. They thought you should be told by her, through me, since you first made the suggestion to her and therefore you would want to know that the arrangement is satisfactory to her. An FBC lawyer is drafting an agreement to be signed by Mr. Wolfe and the other parties."

"Mr. Wolfe hates to sign anything written by a lawyer. Ten to one he won't sign it. He'll insist on dictating it to me, so you might as well give me the details."

She objected. "Then someone else may refuse to sign it."

"Not a chance," I assured her. "The people who have been phoning here all day would sign anything. What's the arrangement?"

"Well, just as you suggested. As you proposed it to Miss Fraser. No one objected to that. What they've been discussing was how to divide it up, and this is what they've agreed on . . ."

As she told it to me I scribbled it in my notebook, and this is how it looked:

	Per cent of expenses	Share of fee
Hi-Spot	50	$10,000
FBC	28	5,500
M. Fraser	15	3,000
White Birch Soap	5	1,000
Sweeties	2	500
	100	$20,000

I called it back to check and then stated, "It suits us if it suits Miss Fraser. Is she satisfied?"

"She agrees to it," Deborah said. "She would have preferred to do it alone, all herself, but under the circumstances that wasn't possible. Yes, she's satisfied."

"Okay. Mr. Wolfe will dictate it, probably in the form of a letter, with copies for all. But that's just a formality and he wants to get started. All we know is what we've read in the papers. According to them there are eight people that the police regard as—uh, possibilities. Their names—"

"I know their names. Including mine."

"Sure you do. Can you have them all here at this office at half past eight this evening?"

"All of them?"

"Yes, ma'am."

"But is that necessary?"

"Mr. Wolfe thinks so. This is him talking through me, to Miss Fraser through you. I ought to warn you, he can be an awful nuisance when a good fee depends on it. Usually when you hire a man to do something he thinks you're the boss. When you hire Wolfe he thinks he's the boss. He's a genius and that's merely one of the ways it shows. You can either take it or fight it. What do you want, just the publicity, or do you want the job done?"

"Don't bully me, Mr. Goodwin. We want the job done. I don't know if I can get Professor Savarese. And that Shepherd girl—she's a bigger nuisance than Mr. Wolfe could ever possibly be."

"Will you get all you can? Half past eight. And keep me informed?"

She said she would. After I had hung up I buzzed Wolfe on the house phone to tell him we had made a sale.

It soon became apparent that we had also bought something. It was only twenty-five to six, less than three-quarters of an hour since I had finished with Deborah Koppel, when the doorbell rang. Sometimes Fritz answers it and sometimes me—usually me, when I'm home and not engaged on something that shouldn't be interrupted. So I marched to the hall and to the front door and pulled it open.

On the stoop was a surprise party. In front was a man-about-town in a topcoat the Duke of Windsor would have worn any day. To his left and rear was a red-faced plump gentleman. Back of them were three more, miscellaneous, carrying an assortment of cases and bags. When I saw what I had to contend with I brought the door with me and held it, leaving only enough of an opening for room for my shoulders.

"We'd like to see Mr. Nero Wolfe," the topcoat said like an old friend.

"He's engaged. I'm Archie Goodwin. Can I help?"

"You certainly can! I'm Fred Owen, in charge of public relations for the Hi-Spot Company." He was pushing a hand at me and I took it. "And this is Mr. Walter B. Anderson, the president of the Hi-Spot Company. May we come in?"

I reached to take the president's hand and still keep my door block intact. "If you don't mind," I said, "it would be a help if you'd give me a rough idea."

"Certainly, glad to! I would have phoned, only this has to be rushed if we're going to make the morning papers. So I just persuaded Mr. Anderson, and collected the photographers, and came. It shouldn't take ten minutes—say a shot of Mr. Anderson looking at Mr. Wolfe as he signs the agreement, or vice versa, and one of them shaking hands, and one of them side by side, bending over in a huddle inspecting some object that can be captioned as a clue—how about that one?"

"Wonderful!" I grinned at him. "But damn it, not today. Mr. Wolfe cut himself shaving, and he's wearing a patch, and vain as he is it would be very risky to aim a camera at him."

That goes to show how a man will degrade himself on account of money. Meaning me. The proper and natural thing to do would have been to kick them off the stoop down the seven steps to the sidewalk, especially the topcoat, and why didn't I do it? Ten grand. Maybe even twenty, for if Hi-Spot had been insulted they might have soured the whole deal.

The effort, including sacrifice of principle, that it took to get them on their way without making them too sore put me in a frame of mind that accounted for my reaction somewhat later, after Wolfe had come down to the office, when I had explained the agreement our clients had come to, and he said:

19

"No. I will not." He was emphatic. "I will not draft or sign an agreement one of the parties to which is that Sweeties."

I knew perfectly well that was reasonable and even noble. But what pinched me was that I had sacrificed principle without hesitation, and here he was refusing to. I glared at him:

"Very well." I stood up. "I resign as of now. You are simply too conceited, too eccentric, and too fat to work for."

"Archie. Sit down."

"No."

"Yes. I am no fatter than I was five years ago. I am considerably more conceited, but so are you, and why the devil shouldn't we be? Some day there will be a crisis. Either you'll get insufferable and I'll fire you, or I'll get insufferable and you'll quit. But this isn't the day and you know it. You also know I would rather become a policeman and take orders from Mr. Cramer than work for anything or anyone called Sweeties. Your performance yesterday and today has been highly satisfactory."

"Don't try to butter me."

"Bosh. I repeat that I am no fatter than I was five years ago. Sit down and get your notebook. We'll put it in the form of a letter, to all of them jointly, and they can initial our copy. We shall ignore Sweeties"—he made a face—"and add that two per cent and that five hundred dollars to the share of the Federal Broadcasting Company."

That was what we did.

By the time Fritz called us to dinner there had been phone calls from Deborah Koppel and others, and the party for the evening was set.

5

THERE are four rooms on the ground floor of Wolfe's old brownstone house on West Thirty-fifth Street not far from the Hudson River. As you enter from the stoop, on your right are an enormous old oak clothes rack with a mirror, the elevator, the stairs, and the door to the dining room. On your left are the doors to the front room, which doesn't get used much, and to the office. The door to the kitchen is at the rear, the far end of the hall.

The office is twice as big as any of the other rooms. It is

actually our living room too, and since Wolfe spends most of his time there you have to allow him his rule regarding furniture and accessories: nothing enters it or stays in it that he doesn't enjoy looking at. He enjoys the contrast between the cherry of his desk and the cardato of his chair, made by Meyer. The bright yellow couch has to be cleaned every two months, but he likes bright yellow. The three-foot globe over by the bookshelves is too big for a room that size, but he likes to look at it. He loves a comfortable chair so much that he won't have any other kind in the place, though he never sits on any but his own.

So that evening at least our guests' fannies were at ease, however the rest of them may have felt. There were nine of them present, six invited and three gate-crashers. Of the eight I had wanted Deborah Koppel to get, Nancylee Shepherd hadn't been asked, and Professor F. O. Savarese couldn't make it. The three gate-crashers were Hi-Spot's president and public relations man, Anderson and Owen, who had previously only got as far as the stoop, and Beech, the FBC vice-president.

At nine o'clock they were all there, all sitting, and all looking at Wolfe. There had been no friction at all except a little brush I had with Anderson. The best chair in the room, not counting Wolfe's, is one of red leather which is kept not far from one end of Wolfe's desk. Soon after entering Anderson had spotted it and squat-claimed it. When I asked him courteously to move to the other side of the room he went rude on me. He said he liked it there.

"But," I said, "this chair, and those, are reserved for the candidates."

"Candidates for what?"

"For top billing in a murder trial. Mr. Wolfe would like them sort of together, so they'll all be under his eye."

"Then arrange them that way."

He wasn't moving. "I can't ask you to show me your stub," I said pointedly, "because this is merely a private house, and you weren't invited, and my only argument is the convenience and pleasure of your host."

He gave me a dirty look but no more words, got up, and went across to the couch. I moved Madeline Fraser to the red leather chair, which gave the other five candidates more elbow room in their semicircle fronting Wolfe's desk. Beech, who had been standing talking to Wolfe, went and took a chair near the end of the couch. Owen had joined his boss, so I had the three gate-crashers off to themselves, which was as it should be.

Wolfe's eyes swept the semicircle, starting at Miss Fraser's end. "You are going to find this tiresome," he said conversationally, "because I'm just starting on this and so shall have to cover details that you're sick of hearing and talking about. All the information I have has come from newspapers, and therefore much of it is doubtless inaccurate and some of it false. How much you'll have to correct me on I don't know."

"It depends a lot," said Nathan Traub with a smile, "on which paper you read."

Traub, the agency man, was the only one of the six I hadn't seen before, having only heard his smooth low-pitched voice on the phone, when he had practically told me that everything had to be cleared through him. He was much younger than I had expected, around my age, but otherwise he was no great surprise. The chief difference between any two advertising executives is that one goes to buy a suit at Brooks Brothers in the morning and the other one goes in the afternoon. It depends on the conference schedule. The suit this Traub had bought was a double-breasted gray which went very well with his dark hair and the healthy color of his cheeks.

"I have read them all." Wolfe's eyes went from left to right again. "I did so when I decided I wanted a job on this case. By the way, I assume you all know who has hired me, and for what?"

There were nods. "We know all about it," Bill Meadows said.

"Good. Then you know why the presence of Mr. Anderson, Mr. Owen, and Mr. Beech is being tolerated. With them here, and of course Miss Fraser, ninety-five per cent of the clients' interest is represented. The only one absent is White Birch Soap."

"They're not absent." Nathan Traub was politely indignant. "I can speak for them."

"I'd rather you'd speak for yourself," Wolfe retorted. "The clients are here to listen, not to speak." He rested his elbows on the arms of his chair and put the tips of his thumbs together. With the gate-crashers put in their places, he went on, "As for you, ladies and gentlemen, this would be much more interesting and stimulating for you if I could begin by saying that my job is to learn which one of you is guilty of murder—and to prove it. Unfortunately we can't have that fillip, since two of the eight—Miss Shepherd and Mr. Savarese didn't come. I am told that Mr. Savarese had an engagement, and there is a certain reluctance about Miss Shepherd that I would like to know more about."

"She's a nosy little chatterbox." From Tully Strong, who had removed his spectacles and was gazing at Wolfe with an intent frown.

"She's a pain in the neck." From Bill Meadows.

Everybody smiled, some nervously, some apparently meaning it.

"I didn't try to get her," Deborah Koppel said. "She wouldn't have come unless Miss Fraser herself had asked her, and I didn't think that was necessary. She hates all the rest of us."

"Why?"

"Because she thinks we keep her away from Miss Fraser."

"Do you?"

"Yes. We try to."

"Not from me too, I hope." Wolfe sighed down to where a strip of his yellow shirt divided his vest from his trousers, and curled his palms and fingers over the ends of his chair arms. "Now. Let's get at this. Usually when I talk I dislike interruptions, but this is an exception. If you disagree with anything I say, or think me in error, say so at once. With that understood:

"Frequently, twice a week or oftener, you consider the problem of guests for Miss Fraser's program. It is in fact a problem, because you want interesting people, famous ones if possible, but they must be willing to submit to the indignity of lending their presence, and their assent by silence, if nothing more, to the preposterous statements made by Miss Fraser and Mr. Meadows regarding the products they advertise. Recently—"

"What's undignified about it?"

"There are no preposterous statements!"

"What's this got to do with what we're paying you for?"

"You disagree." Wolfe was unruffled. "I asked for it. Archie, include it in your notes that Mr. Traub and Mr. Strong disagree. You may ignore Mr. Owen's protest, since my invitation to interrupt did not extend to him."

He took in the semicircle again. "Recently a suggestion was made that you corral, as a guest, a man who sells tips on horse races. I understand that your memories differ as to when that suggestion was first made."

Madeline Fraser said, "It's been discussed off and on for over a year."

23

"I've always been dead against it," Tully Strong asserted.

Deborah Koppel smiled. "Mr. Strong thought it would be improper. He thinks the program should never offend anybody, which is impossible. Anything and everything offends somebody."

"What changed your mind, Mr. Strong?"

"Two things," said the secretary of the Sponsors' Council. "First, we got the idea of having the audience vote on it—the air audience—and out of over fourteen thousand letters ninety-two point six per cent were in favor. Second, one of the letters was from an assistant professor of mathematics at Columbia University, suggesting that the second guest on the program should be him, or some other professor, who could speak as an expert on the law of averages. That gave it a different slant entirely, and I was for it. Nat Traub, for the agency, was still against it."

"And I still am," Traub declared. "Can you blame me?"

"So," Wolfe asked Strong. "Mr. Traub was a minority of one?"

"That's right. We went ahead. Miss Vance, who does research for the program in addition to writing scripts, got up a list of prospects. I was surprised to find, and the others were too, that more than thirty tip sheets of various kinds are published in New York alone. We boiled it down to five and they were contacted."

I should have warned them that the use of "contact" as a verb was not permitted in that office. Now Wolfe would have it in for him.

Wolfe frowned. "All five were invited?"

"Oh, no. Appointments were made for them to see Miss Fraser—the publishers of them. She had to find out which one was most likely to go over on the air and not pull something that would hurt the program. The final choice was left to her."

"How were the five selected?"

"Scientifically. The length of time they had been in business, the quality of paper and printing of the sheets, the opinions of sports writers, things like that."

"Who was the scientist? You?"

"No . . . I don't know . . ."

"I was," a firm quiet voice stated. It was Elinor Vance. I had put her in the chair nearest mine because Wolfe isn't the only one who likes to have things around that he enjoys looking at. Obviously she hadn't caught up on sleep yet, and every so often she had to clamp her teeth to keep her chin from quivering, but she was the only one there who could conceivably have made me remember that I was not primarily a detective, but a man. I was curious how her brown eyes would look if and when they got fun in them again some day. She was going on:

"First I took out those that were plainly impossible, more than half of them, and then I talked it over with Miss Koppel and Mr. Meadows, and I think one or two others—I guess Mr. Strong—yes, I'm sure I did—but it was me more than them. I picked the five names."

"And they all came to see Miss Fraser?"

"Four of them did. One of them was out of town—in Florida."

Wolfe's gaze went to the left. "And you, Miss Fraser, chose Mr. Cyril Orchard from those four?"

She nodded. "Yes."

"How did you do that? Scientifically?"

"No." She smiled. "There's nothing scientific about me. He seemed fairly intelligent, and he had much the best voice of the four and was the best talker, and I liked the name of his sheet, *Track Almanac*—and then I guess I was a little snobbish about it too. His sheet was the most expensive—ten dollars a week."

"Those were the considerations that led you to select him?"

"Yes."

"You had never seen or heard of him before he came to see you as one of the four?"

"I hadn't seen him, but I had heard of him, and I had seen his sheet."

"Oh?" Wolfe's eyes went half shut. "You had?"

"Yes, about a month before that, maybe longer, when the question of having a tipster on the program had come up again, I had subscribed to some of the sheets—three or four of them—to see what they were like. Not in my name, of course. Things like that are done in my manager's name—Miss Koppel. One of them was this *Track Almanac*."

"How did you happen to choose that one?"

"My God, I don't know!" Madeline Fraser's eyes flashed momentarily with irritation. "Do you remember, Debby?"

Deborah shook her head. "I think we phoned somebody."

"The New York State Racing Commission," Bill Meadows offered sarcastically.

"Well." Wolfe leaned forward to push a button on his desk. "I'm going to have some beer. Aren't some of you thirsty?"

That called for an intermission. No one had accepted a previous offer of liquids I had made, but now they made it unanimous in the affirmative, and I got busy at the table at the far wall, already equipped. Two of them joined Wolfe with the beer, brought by Fritz from the kitchen, and the others suited their fancy. I had suggested to Wolfe that it would be fitting to have a case of Hi-Spot in a prominent place on the table, but he had merely snorted. On such occasions he always insisted that a red wine and a chilled white wine must be among those present. Usually they had no takers, but this time there were two, Miss Koppel and Traub, who went for the Montrachet; and, being strongly in favor of the way its taste insists on sneaking all over the inside of your head, I helped out with it. There is only one trouble about serving assorted drinks to a bunch of people in the office on business. I maintain that it is a legitimate item for the expense account for the clients, and Wolfe says no, that what anyone eats or drinks in his house is on him. Another eccentricity. Also he insists that they must all have stands or tables at their elbows for their drinks.

So they did.

6

WOLFE, for whom the first bottle of beer is merely a preamble, filled his glass from the second bottle, put the bottle down, and leaned back.

"What I've been after," he said in his conversational tone again, "is how that particular individual, Mr. Cyril Orchard, became a guest on that program. The conclusion from the newspaper accounts is that none of you, including Miss Shepherd and Mr. Savarese, knew him from Adam. But he was murdered. Later I'll discuss this with you severally, but for now I'll just put it to all of you: had you had any dealings with, or connection with, or knowledge of, Cyril Orchard prior to his appearance on that program? Other than what I have just been told?"

Starting with Madeline Fraser, he got either a no or a shake of the head from each of the six.

He grunted. "I assume," he said, "that the police have unearthed no contradiction to any of your negatives, since if they had you would hardly be foolish enough to try to hold to them with me. My whole approach to this matter is quite different from what it would be if I didn't know that the police have spent seven days and nights working on it. They have been after you, and they have their training and talents; also they have authority and a thousand men—twenty thousand. The question is whether their methods and abilities are up to this job; all I can do is use my own."

Wolfe came forward to drink beer, used his handkerchief on his lips, and leaned back again.

"But I need to know what happened—from you, not the newspapers. We now have you in the broadcasting studio Tuesday morning, a week ago today. The two guests—Mr. Cyril Orchard and Professor Savarese—have arrived. It is a quarter to eleven. The rest of you are there, at or near the table which holds the microphones. Seated at one side of the narrow table are Miss Fraser and Professor Savarese; across from them, facing them, are Mr. Orchard and Mr. Meadows. Voice levels are being taken. About twenty feet from the table is the first row of chairs provided for the studio audience That audience consists of some two hundred people, nearly all women, many of whom, devoted followers of Miss Fraser, frequently attend the broadcasts. Is that picture correct—not approximately correct, but correct?"

They nodded. "Nothing wrong with it," Bill Meadows said.

"Many of them," Miss Fraser stated, "would come much oftener if they could get tickets. There are always twice as many applications for tickets as we can supply."

"No doubt." Wolfe growled. He had shown great restraint, not telling her how dangerous she was. "But the applicants who didn't get tickets, not being there, do not concern us. An essential element of the picture which I haven't mentioned is not yet visible. Behind the closed door of an electric refrigerator over against the wall are eight bottles of Hi-Spot. How did they get there?"

An answer came from the couch, from Fred Owen. "We always have three or four cases in the studio, in a locked cab——"

"If you please, Mr. Owen." Wolfe wiggled a finger at him. "I want to hear as much as I can of the voices of these six people."

"They were there in the studio," Tully Strong said. "In a cabinet It's kept locked because if it wasn't they wouldn't be there long."

"Who had taken the eight bottles from the cabinet and put them in the refrigerator?"

"I had." It was Elinor Vance, and I looked up from my

notebook for another glance at her. "That's one of my chores every broadcast."

One trouble with her, I thought, is overwork. Script writer, researcher, bartender—what else?

"You can't carry eight bottles," Wolfe remarked, "at one time."

"I know I can't, so I took four and then went back for four more."

"Leaving the cabinet unlocked—no." Wolfe stopped himself. "Those refinements will have to wait." His eyes passed along the line again. "So there they are, in the refrigerator.— By the way, I understand that the presence at the broadcast of all but one of you was routine and customary. The exception was you, Mr. Traub. You very rarely attend. What were you there for?"

"Because I was jittery, Mr. Wolfe." Traub's advertising smile and smooth low-pitched voice showed no resentment at being singled out. "I still thought having a race tout on the program was a mistake, and I wanted to be on hand."

"You thought there was no telling what Mr. Orchard might say?"

"I knew nothing about Orchard. I thought the whole idea was a stinker."

"If you mean the whole idea of the program, I agree—but that's not what we're trying to decide. We'll go on with the broadcast. First, one more piece of the picture. Where are the glasses they're going to drink from?"

"On a tray at the end of the table," Deborah Koppel said.

"The broadcasting table? Where they're seated at the microphones?"

"Yes."

"Who put them there?"

"That girl, Nancylee Shepherd. The only way to keep her back of the line would be to tie her up. Or of course not let her in, and Miss Fraser will not permit that. She organized the biggest Fraser Girls' Club in the country. So we—"

The phone rang. I reached for it and muttered into it.

"Mr. Bluff," I told Wolfe, using one of my fifteen aliases for the caller. Wolfe got his receiver to his ear, giving me a signal to stay on.

"Yes, Mr. Cramer?"

Cramer's sarcastic voice sounded as if he had a cigar stuck in his mouth, as he probably had. "How are you coming up there?"

"Slowly. Not really started yet."

"That's too bad, since no one's paying you on the Orchard case. So you told me yesterday."

"This is today. Tomorrow's paper will tell you all about it. I'm sorry, Mr. Cramer, but I'm busy."

"You certainly are, from the reports I've got here. Which one is your client?"

"You'll see it in the paper."

"Then there's no reason—"

"Yes. There is. That I'm extremely busy and exactly a week behind you. Good-by, sir."

Wolfe's tone and his manner of hanging up got a reaction from the gate-crashers. Mr. Walter B. Anderson, the Hi-Spot president, demanded to know if the caller had been Police Inspector Cramer, and, told that it was, got critical. His position was that Wolfe should not have been rude to the Inspector. It was bad tactics and bad manners. Wolfe, not bothering to draw his sword, brushed him aside with a couple of words, but Anderson leaped for his throat. He had not yet, he said, signed any agreement, and if that was going to be Wolfe's attitude maybe he wouldn't.

"Indeed." Wolfe's brows went up a sixteenth of an inch. "Then you'd better notify the press immediately. Do you want to use the phone?"

"By God, I wish I could. I have a right to—"

"You have no right whatever, Mr. Anderson, except to pay your share of my fee if I earn it. You are here in my office on sufferance. Confound it, I am undertaking to solve a problem that has Mr. Cramer so nonplused that he desperately wants a hint from me before I've even begun. He doesn't mind my rudeness; he's so accustomed to it that if I were affable he'd haul me in as a material witness. Are you going to use the phone?"

"You know damn well I'm not."

"I wish you were. The better I see this picture the less I like it." Wolfe went back to the line of candidates. "You say, Miss Koppel, that this adolescent busybody, Miss Shepherd, put the tray of glasses on the table?"

"Yes, she—"

"She took them from me," Elinor Vance put in, "when I got them from the cabinet. She was right there with her hand out and I let her take them."

"The locked cabinet that the Hi-Spot is kept in?"

"Yes."

"And the glasses are heavy and dark blue, quite opaque so that anything in them is invisible?"

29

"Yes."

"You didn't look into them from the top?"

"No."

"If one of them had something inside you wouldn't have seen it?"

"No." Elinor went on, "If you think my answers are short and quick, that's because I've already answered these questions, and many others, hundreds of times. I could answer them in my sleep."

Wolfe nodded. "Of course. So now we have the bottles in the refrigerator and the glasses on the table, and the program is on the air. For forty minutes it went smoothly. The two guests did well. None of Mr. Traub's fears were realized."

"It was one of the best broadcasts of the year," Miss Fraser said.

"Exceptional," Tully Strong declared. "There were thirty-two studio laughs in the first half hour."

"How did you like the second half?" Traub asked pointedly.

"We're coming to it." Wolfe sighed. "Well, here we are. The moment arrives when Hi-Spot is to be poured, drunk, and eulogized. Who brought it from the refrigerator? You again, Miss Vance?"

"No, me," Bill Meadows said. "It's part of the show for the mikes, me pushing back my chair, walking, opening the refrigerator door and closing it, and coming back with the bottles. Then someone—"

"There were eight bottles in the refrigerator. How many did you get?"

"Four."

"How did you decide which ones?"

"I didn't decide. I always just take the four in front. You realize that all Hi-Spot bottles are exactly alike. There wouldn't be any way to tell them apart, so how would I decide?"

"I couldn't say. Anyway, you didn't?"

"No. As I said, I simply took the four bottles that were nearest to me. That's natural."

"So it is. And carried them to the table and removed the caps?"

"I took them to the table, but about removing the caps, that's something we don't quite agree on. We agree that I didn't do it, because I put them on the table as usual and then got back into my chair, quick, to get on the mike. Someone else always takes the caps from the bottles, not always the same one, and that day Debby—Miss Koppel was right there, and Miss Vance, and Strong, and Traub. I was on the mike and didn't see who removed the caps. The action there is a little tight and needs help, with taking off the caps, pouring into the glasses, and getting the glasses passed around—and the bottles have to be passed around too."

"Who does the passing?"

"Oh, someone—or, rather, more than one. You know, they just get passed—the glasses and bottles both. After pouring into the glasses the bottles are still about half full, so the bottles are passed too."

"Who did the pouring and passing that day?"

Bill Meadows hesitated. "That's what we don't agree about." He was not at ease. "As I said, they were all right there—Miss Koppel and Miss Vance, and Strong and Traub. That's why it was confusing."

"Confusing or not," Wolfe said testily, "it should be possible to remember what happened, so simple a thing as that. This is the detail where, above all others, clarity is essential. We know that Mr. Orchard got the bottle and glass which contained the cyanide, because he drank enough of it to kill him. But we do not know, at least I don't, whether he got it by a whim of circumstance or by the deliberate maneuver of one or more of those present. Obviously that's a vital point. That glass and bottle were placed in front of Mr. Orchard by somebody—not this one, or this one, but that one. Who put it there?"

Wolfe's gaze went along the line. They all met it. No one had anything to say, but neither was anyone impelled to look somewhere else. Finally Tully Strong, who had his spectacles back on, spoke:

"We simply don't remember, Mr. Wolfe."

"Pfui." Wolfe was disgusted. "Certainly you remember. No wonder Mr. Cramer has got nowhere. You're lying, every one of you."

"No," Miss Fraser objected. "They're not lying really."

"The wrong pronoun," Wolfe snapped at her. "My comment included you, Miss Fraser."

She smiled at him. "You may include me if you like, but I don't. It's like this. These people are not only associated with one another in connection with my program, they are friends. Of course they have arguments—there's always bound to be some friction when two people are often together, let alone five or six—but they are friends and they like one another." Her timing and inflections were as good as if she had been on the air. "This is a terrible thing, a horrible thing, and we all knew it was the minute the doctor came and looked at him, and then looked up and said nothing should be touched and no one should leave. So could you really expect one of them to say—or, since you include me, could you expect one of us to say—*yes, I gave him the glass with poison in it?*"

"What was left in the bottle was also poisoned."

"All right, the bottle too. Or could you expect one of us to say, *yes, I saw my friend give him the glass and bottle?* And name the friend?"

"Then you're agreeing with me. That you're all lying."

"Not at all." Miss Fraser was too earnest to smile now. "The pouring and passing the glasses and bottles was commonplace routine, and there was no reason for us to notice details enough to keep them in our minds at all. Then came that overwhelming shock, and the confusion, and later came the police, and the strain and tension of it, and we just didn't remember. That isn't the least bit surprising. What would surprise me would be if someone did remember, for instance if Mr. Traub said positively that Mr. Strong put that glass and bottle in front of Mr. Orchard, it would merely prove that Mr. Traub hates Mr. Strong, and that would surprise me because I don't believe that any one of us hates another one."

"Nor," Wolfe murmured dryly, "that any of you hated Mr. Orchard—or wanted to kill him."

"Who on earth could have wanted to kill that man?"

"I don't know. That's what I've been hired to find out—provided the poison reached its intended destination. You say you're not surprised, but I am. I'm surprised the police haven't locked you all up."

"They damn near did," Traub said grimly.

"I certainly thought they would arrest me," Madeline Fraser declared. "That was what was in my mind—it was all that was in my mind—as soon as I heard the doctor say cyanide. Not who had given him that glass and bottle, not even what the effect would be on my program, but the death of my husband. He died of cyanide poisoning six years ago."

Wolfe nodded. "The papers haven't neglected that. It was what leaped first to your mind?"

"Yes, when I heard the doctor say cyanide. I suppose you wouldn't understand—or perhaps you would—anyway it did."

"It did to mine too," Deborah Koppel interposed, in a tone that implied that someone had been accused of something.

32

"Miss Fraser's husband was my brother. I saw him just after he died. Then that day I saw Cyril Orchard, and—" She stopped. Having her in profile, I couldn't see her eyes, but I saw her clasped hands. In a moment she went on, "Yes, it came to my mind."

Wolfe stirred impatiently. "Well. I won't pretend that I'm exasperated that you're such good friends that you haven't been able to remember what happened. If you had, and had told the police, I might not have this job." He glanced at the clock on the wall. "It's after eleven. I had thought it barely possible that I might get a wedge into a crack by getting you here together, but it seems hopeless. You're much too fond of one another. Our time has been completely wasted. I haven't got a thing, not a microscopic morsel, that I hadn't already got from the papers. I may never get anything, but I intend to try. Which of you will spend the night here with me? Not all the night; probably four or five hours. I shall need that long, more or less, with each of you, and I would like to start now. Which of you will stay?"

There were no eager volunteers.

"My Lord!" Elinor Vance protested. "Over and over and over again."

"My clients," Wolfe said, "are your employer, your network, and your sponsors. Mr. Meadows?"

"I've got to take Miss Fraser home," Bill objected. "I could come back."

"I'll take her," Tully Strong offered.

"That's foolish." Deborah Koppel was annoyed. "I live only a block away and we'll take a taxi together."

"I'll go with you," Elinor Vance suggested. "I'll drop you and keep the taxi on uptown."

"I'll ride with you," Tully Strong insisted.

"But you live in the Village!"

"Count me in," Bill Meadows said stubbornly. "I can be back here in twenty minutes. Thank God tomorrow's Wednesday."

"This is all unnecessary," the president of Hi-Spot broke in with authority. He had left the couch and was among the candidates, who were also on their feet. "My car is outside and I can take all of you who are going uptown. You can stay here with Wolfe, Meadows." He turned and stepped to the desk. "Mr. Wolfe, I haven't been greatly impressed this evening. Hardly at all impressed."

"Neither have I," Wolfe agreed. "It's a dreary outlook. I would prefer to abandon it, but you and I are both committed by that press release." Seeing that some of them were heading for the hall, he raised his voice. "If you please? A moment. I would like to make appointments. One of you tomorrow from eleven to one, another from two to four, another in the evening from eight-thirty to twelve, and another from midnight on. Will you decide on that before you go?"

They did so, with me helping them and making notes of the decisions. It took a little discussion, but they were such good friends that there was no argument. The only thing that soured the leave-taking at all was when Owen made an opportunity to pass me a crack about no patch or cut being visible on Wolfe's face. He might at least have had the decency to let it lay.

"I said nothing about his face," I told him coldly. "I said he cut himself shaving. He shaves his legs. I understood you wanted him in kilts for the pictures."

Owen was too offended to speak. Utterly devoid of a sense of humor.

When the others had gone Bill Meadows was honored with the red leather chair. On a low table at his elbow I put a replenished glass, and Fritz put a tray holding three sandwiches made with his own bread, one of minced rabbit meat, one of corned beef, and one of Georgia country ham. I arranged myself at my desk with my notebook, a plate of sandwiches to match Bill's, a pitcher of milk and a glass. Wolfe had only beer. He never eats between dinner and breakfast. If he did he never would be able to say he is no fatter than he was five years ago, which isn't true anyhow.

In a way it's a pleasure to watch Wolfe doing a complete overhaul on a man, or a woman either, and in another way it's enough to make you grit your teeth. When you know exactly what he's after and he's sneaking up on it without the slightest sound to alarm the victim, it's a joy to be there. But when he's after nothing in particular, or if he is you don't know what, and he pokes in this hole a while and then tries another one, and then goes back to the first one, and as far as you can see is getting absolutely nowhere, and the hours go by, and your sandwiches and milk are all gone long ago, sooner or later the time comes when you don't even bother to get a hand in front of your yawns, let alone swallow them.

If, at four o'clock that Wednesday morning, Wolfe had once more started in on Bill Meadows about his connections with people who bet on horse races, or about the favorite topics of conversation among the people we were interested in when they weren't talking shop, or about how he got into broadcasting and did he like it much, I would either have thrown my notebook at him or gone to the kitchen for more milk. But he didn't. He pushed back his chair and manipulated himself to his feet. If anyone wants to know what I had in the notebook he can come to the office any time I'm not busy and I'll read it to him for a dollar a page, but he would be throwing his money away at any price.

I ushered Bill out. When I returned to the office Fritz was there tidying up. He never goes to bed until after Wolfe does. He asked me:

"Was the corned beef juicy, Archie?"

"Good God," I demanded, "do you expect me to remember that far back? That was days ago." I went to spin the knob on the safe and jiggle the handle, remarking to Wolfe:

"It seems we're still in the paddock, not even at the starting post. Who do you want in the morning? Saul and Orrie and Fred and Johnny? For what? Why not have them tail Mr. Anderson?"

"I do not intend," Wolfe said glumly, "to start spending money until I know what I want to buy—not even our clients' money. If this poisoner is going to be exposed by such activities as investigation of sales of potassium cyanide or of sources of it available to these people, it is up to Mr. Cramer and his twenty thousand men. Doubtless they have already done about all they can in those directions, and many others, or he wouldn't have phoned me squealing for help. The only person I want to see in the morning is—who is it? Who's coming at eleven?"

"Debby. Miss Koppel."

"You might have taken the men first, on the off chance that we'd have it before we got to the women." He was at the door to the hall. "Good night."

7

If, THIRTY-THREE hours later, at lunch time on Thursday, anyone had wanted to know how things were shapping up, he could have satisfied his curiosity by looking in the dining room and observing Wolfe's behavior at the midday meal, which consisted of corn fritters with autumn honey, sausages, and a bowl of salad. At meals he is always expansive, talkative, and good-humored, but throughout that one he was grim, sullen, and peevish. Fritz was worried stiff.

Wednesday we had entertained Miss Koppel from eleven to one, Miss Fraser from two to four, Miss Vance from eight-thirty in the evening until after eleven, and Nathan Traub from midnight on; and Tully Strong Thursday morning from eleven until lunch time.

We had got hundreds of notebook pages of nothing.

Gaps had of course been filled in, but with what? We even had confessions, but of what? Bill Meadows and Nat Traub both confessed that they frequently bet on horse races. Elinor Vance confessed that her brother was an electroplater, and that she was aware that he constantly used materials which contained cyanide. Madeline Fraser confessed that it was hard to believe that anyone would have put poison into one of the bottles without caring a damn which one of the four broadcasters it got served to. Tully Strong confessed that the police had found his fingerprints on all four of the bottles, and accounted for them by explaining that while the doctor had been kneeling to examine Cyril Orchard, he, Strong, had been horrified by the possibility that there had been something wrong with a bottle of Hi-Spot, the product of the most important sponsor on the Council. In a panic he had seized the four bottles, with the idiotic notion of caching them somewhere, and Miss Fraser and Traub had taken them from him and replaced them on the table. That was a particularly neat confession, since it explained why the cops had got nowhere from prints on the bottles.

Deborah Koppel confessed that she knew a good deal about cyanides, their uses, effects, symptoms, doses, and accessibility, because she had read up on them after the death of her brother six years ago. In all the sessions those were the only two times Wolfe got really disagreeable, when he was asking about the death of Lawrence Koppel—first with Deborah, the sister, and then with Madeline Fraser, the widow. The details had of course been pie for the newspapers during the past week, on account of the coincidence of the cyanide, and one of the tabloids had even gone so far as to run a piece by an expert, discussing whether it had really been suicide, though there hadn't been the slightest question about it at the time or at any time since.

But that wasn't the aspect that Wolfe was disagreeable about. Lawrence Koppel's death had occurred at his home in a little town in Michigan called Fleetville, and what Wolfe wanted to know was whether there had been anyone in or near Fleetville who was named Orchard, or who had relatives named Orchard, or who had later changed his name to Orchard. I don't know how it had entered his head that that was a hot idea, but he certainly wrung it dry and kept going back to it for another squeeze. He spent so much time on it with Madeline Fraser that four o'clock, the hour of his afternoon date with the orchids, came before he had asked her anything at all about horse races.

The interviews with those five were not all that happened that day and night and morning. Wolfe and I had discussions, of the numerous ways in which a determined and intelligent person can get his hands on a supply of cyanide, of the easy access to the bottles in the refrigerator in the broadcasting studio, of the advisability of trying to get Inspector Cramer or Sergeant Purley Stebbins to cough up some data on things like fingerprints. That got us exactly as far as the interviews did. Then there were two more phone calls from Cramer, and some from Lon Cohen and various others; and there was the little detail of arranging for Professor F. O. Savarese to pay us a visit.

Also the matter of arranging for Nancylee Shepherd to come and be processed, but on that we were temporarily stymied. We knew all about her: she was sixteen, she lived with her parents at 829 Wixley Avenue in the Bronx, she had light yellow hair and gray eyes, and her father worked in a storage warehouse. They had no phone, so at four Wednesday, when Miss Fraser had left and Wolfe had gone up to the plants, I got the car from the garage and drove to the Bronx.

829 Wixley Avenue was the kind of apartment house where people live not because they want to, but because they

have to. It should have been ashamed of itself and probably was. There was no click when I pushed the button marked Shepherd, so I went to the basement and dug up the janitor. He harmonized well with the building. He said I was way behind time if I expected to get any effective results—that's what he said—pushing the Shepherd button. They had been gone three days now. No, not the whole family, Mrs. Shepherd and the girl. He didn't know where they had gone, and neither did anyone else around there. Some thought they had skipped, and some thought the cops had 'em. He personally thought they might be dead. No, not Mr. Shepherd too. He came home from work every afternoon a little after five, and left every morning at half past six.

A glance at my wrist showing me ten to five, I offered the animal a buck to stick around the front and give me a sign when Shepherd showed up, and the look in his eye told me that I had wasted at least four bits of the clients' money.

It wasn't a long wait. When Shepherd appeared I saw that it wouldn't have been necessary to keep the janitor away from his work, for from the line of the eyebrows it was about as far up to the beginning of his hair as it was down to the point of his chin, and a sketchy description would have been enough. Whoever designs the faces had lost all sense of proportion. As he was about to enter the vestibule I got in front of him and asked without the faintest touch of condescension:

"Mr. Shepherd?"

"Get out," he snarled.

"My name's Goodwin and I'm working for Miss Madeline Fraser. I understand your wife and daughter—"

"Get out!"

"But I only want—"

"Get out!"

He didn't put a hand on me or shoulder me, and I can't understand yet how he got past me to the vestibule without friction, but he did, and got his key in the door. There were of course a dozen possible courses for me, anything from grabbing his coat and holding on to plugging him in the jaw, but while that would have given me emotional release it wouldn't have got what I wanted. It was plain that as long as he was conscious he wasn't going to tell me where Nancylee was, and unconscious he couldn't. I passed.

I drove back down to Thirty-fifth Street, left the car at the curb, went in to the office, and dialed Madeline Fraser's number. Deborah Koppel answered, and I asked her:

"Did you folks know that Nancylee has left home? With her mother?"

Yes, she said, they knew that.

"You didn't mention it when you were here this morning. Neither did Miss Fraser this afternoon."

"There was no reason to mention it, was there? We weren't asked."

"You were asked about Nancylee, both of you."

"But not if she had left home or where she is."

"Then may I ask you now? Where is she?"

"I don't know."

"Does Miss Fraser?"

"No. None of us knows."

"How did you know she was gone?"

"She phoned Miss Fraser and told her she was going."

"When was that?"

"That was . . . that was Sunday."

"She didn't say where she was going?"

"No."

That was best I could get. When I was through trying and had hung up, I sat and considered. There was a chance that Purley Stebbins of Homicide would be in the mood for tossing me a bone, since Cramer had been spending nickels on us, but if I asked him for it he would want to make it a trade, and I had nothing to offer. So when I reached for the phone again it wasn't that number, but the *Gazette's*, that I dialed.

Lon Cohen immediately got personal. Where, he wanted to know, had I got the idea that an open press release made an entry in my credit column?

I poohed him. "Some day, chum, you'll get a lulu. Say in about six months, the way we're going. A newspaper is supposed to render public service, and I want some. Did you know that Nancylee Shepherd and her mother have blown?"

"Certainly. The father got sore because she was mixed up in a murder case. He damn near killed two photographers. Father has character."

"Yeah, I've met Father. What did he do with his wife and daughter, bury them?"

"Shipped 'em out of town. With Cramer's permission, as we got it here, and of course Cramer knew where but wasn't giving out. Naturally we thought it an outrage. Is the great public, are the American people, to be deceived and kept in ignorance? No. You must have had a hunch, because we just got it here—it came in less than an hour ago. Nancylee and her mother are at the Ambassador in Atlantic City, sitting room, bedroom, and bath."

"You don't say. Paid for by?"

He didn't know. He agreed that it was intolerable that the American people, of whom I was one, should be uninformed on so vital a point, and before he hung up he said he would certainly do something about it.

When Wolfe came down to the office I reported developments. At that time we still had three more to overhaul, but it was already apparent that we were going to need all we could get, so Wolfe told me to get Saul Panzer on the phone. Saul wasn't in, but an hour later he called back.

Saul Panzer free-lances. He has no office and doesn't need one. He is so good that he demands, and gets, double the market, and any day of the week he gets so many offers that he can pick as he pleases. I have never known him to turn Wolfe down except when he was so tied up he couldn't shake loose.

He took this on. He would take a train to Atlantic City that evening, sleep there, and in the morning persuade Mrs. Shepherd to let Nancylee come to New York for a talk with Wolfe. He would bring her, with Mother if necessary.

As Wolfe was finishing with Saul, Fritz entered with a tray. I looked at him with surprise, since Wolfe seldom takes on beer during the hour preceding dinner, but then, as he put the tray on the desk, I saw it wasn't beer. It was a bottle of Hi-Spot, with three glasses. Instead of turning to leave, Fritz stood by.

"It may be too cold," Fritz suggested.

With a glance of supercilious distaste at the bottle, Wolfe got the opener from his top drawer, removed the cap, and started pouring.

"It seems to me," I remarked, "like a useless sacrifice. Why suffer? If Orchard had never drunk Hi-Spot before he wouldn't know whether it tasted right or not, and even if he didn't like it they were on the air and just for politeness he would have gulped some down." I took the glass that Fritz handed me, a third full. "Anyway he drank enough to kill him, so what does it matter what we think?"

"He may have drunk it before." Wolfe held the glass to his nose, sniffed, and made a face. "At any rate, the murderer had to assume that he might have. Would the difference in taste be too great a hazard?"

"I see." I sipped. "Not so bad." I sipped again. "The only

way we can really tell is to drink this and then drink some cyanide. Have you got some?"

"Don't bubble, Archie." Wolfe put his glass down after two little tastes. "Good heavens. What the devil is in it, Fritz?"

Fritz shook his head. "Ipecac?" he guessed. "Horehound? Would you like some sherry?"

"No. Water. I'll get it." Wolfe got up, marched to the hall, and turned toward the kitchen. He believes in some good healthy exercise before dinner.

That evening, Wednesday, our victims were first Elinor Vance and then Nathan Traub. It was more than three hours after midnight when Wolfe finally let Traub go, which made two nights in a row.

Thursday morning at eleven we started on Tully Strong. In the middle of it, right at noon, there was a phone call from Saul Panzer. Wolfe took it, giving me the sign to stay on. I knew from the tone of Saul's voice, just pronouncing my name, that he had no bacon.

"I'm at the Atlantic City railroad station," Saul said, "and I can either catch a train to New York in twenty minutes or go jump in the ocean, whichever you advise. I couldn't get to Mrs. Shepherd just by asking, so I tried a trick but it didn't work. Finally she and the daughter came down to the hotel lobby, but I thought it would be better to wait until they came outside, if they came, and they did. My approach was one that has worked a thousand times, but it didn't with her. She called a cop and wanted him to arrest me for annoying her. I made another try later, on the phone again, but four words was as far as I got. Now it's no use. This is the third time I've flopped on you in ten years, and that's too often. I don't want you to pay me, not even expenses."

"Nonsense." Wolfe never gets riled with Saul. "You can give me the details later, if there are any I should have. Will you reach New York in time to come to the office at six o'clock?"

"Yes."

"Good. Do that."

Wolfe resumed with Traub. As I have already mentioned, the climax of that two hours' hard work was when Traub confessed that he frequently bet on horse races. As soon as he had gone Wolfe and I went to the dining room for the lunch previously described, corn fritters with autumn honey, sausages, and a bowl of salad. Of course what added to his

41

misery was the fact that Savarese was expected at two o'clock, because he likes to have the duration of a meal determined solely by the inclination of him and the meal, not by some extraneous phenomenon like the sound of a doorbell.

But the bell rang right on the dot.

8

You HAVE heard of the exception that proves the rule. Professor F. O. Savarese was it.

The accepted rule is that an Italian is dark and, if not actually a runt, at least not tall; that a professor is dry and pedantic, with eye trouble; and that a mathematician really lives in the stratosphere and is here just visiting relatives. Well, Savarese was an Italian-American professor of mathematics, but he was big and blond and buoyant, two inches taller than me, and he came breezing in like a March morning wind.

He spent the first twenty minutes telling Wolfe and me how fascinating and practical it would be to work out a set of mathematical formulas that could be used in the detective business. His favorite branch of mathematics, he said, was the one that dealt with the objective numerical measurement of probability. Very well. What was any detective work, any kind at all, but the objective measurement of probability? All he proposed to do was to add the word *numerical*, not as a substitute or replacement, but as an ally and reinforcement.

"I'll show you what I mean," he offered. "May I have paper and pencil?"

He had bounded over to me before I could even uncross my legs, took the pad and pencil I handed him, and bounded back to the red leather chair. When the pencil had jitterbugged on the pad for half a minute he tore off the top sheet and slid it across the desk to Wolfe, then went to work on the next sheet and in a moment tore that off and leaped to me with it.

"You should each have one," he said, "so you can follow me."

I wouldn't try to pretend I could put it down from

memory, but I still have both of those sheets, in the folder marked ORCHARD, and this is what is on them:

$$u = \frac{1}{V_{2\pi} \cdot D} \left\{ 1 - \frac{1}{2} k \left(\frac{X}{D} - \frac{1}{3} \frac{X^3}{D^3} \right) \right\} e^{-\frac{1}{2} X^2/D^2}$$

"That," Savarese said, his whole face smiling with eager interest and friendliness and desire to help, "is the second approximation of the normal law of error, sometimes called the generalized law of error. Let's apply it to the simplest kind of detective problem, say the question which one of three servants in a house stole a diamond ring from a locked drawer. I should explain that X is the deviation from the mean, D is the standard deviation, k is—"

"Please!" Wolfe had to make it next door to a bellow, and did. "What are you trying to do, change the subject?"

"No." Savarese looked surprised and a little hurt. "Am I? What was the subject?"

"The death of Mr. Cyril Orchard and your connection with it."

"Oh. Of course." He smiled apologetically and spread his hands, palms up. "Perhaps later? It is one of my favorite ideas, the application of the mathematical laws of probability and error to detective problems, and a chance to discuss it with you is a golden opportunity."

"Another time. Meanwhile"—Wolfe tapped the generalized law of error with a finger tip—"I'll keep this. Which one of the people at that broadcast placed that glass and bottle in front of Mr. Orchard?"

"I don't know. I'm going to find it very interesting to compare your handling of me with the way the police did it. What you're trying to do, of course, is to proceed from probability toward certainty, as close as you can get. Say you start, as you see it, with one chance in five that I poisoned Orchard. Assuming that you have no subjective bias, your purpose is to move as rapidly as possible from that position, and you don't care which direction. Anything I say or do will move you one way or the other. If one way, the one-in-five will become one-in-four, one-in-three, and so on until it becomes one-in-one and a minute fraction, which will be close enough to affirmative certainty so that you will say you know that I killed Orchard. If it goes the other way, your one-in-five will become one-in-ten, one-in-one-hundred, one-in-one-thousand; and when it gets to one-in-ten-billion you will be close enough to negative certainty so that you will say you know that I did not kill Orchard. There is a formula—"

"No doubt." Wolfe was controlling himself very well. "If you want to compare me with the police you'll have to let me get a word in now and then. Had you ever seen Mr. Orchard before the day of the broadcast?"

"Oh, yes, six times. The first time was thirteen months earlier, in February 1947. You're going to find me remarkably exact, since the police have had me over all this, back and forth. I might as well give you everything I can that will move you toward affirmative certainty, since subjectively you would prefer that direction. Shall I do that?"

"By all means."

"I thought that would appeal to you. As a mathematician I have always been interested in the application of the calculation of probabilities to the various forms of gambling. The genesis of normal distributions—"

"Not now," Wolfe said sharply.

"Oh—of course not. There are reasons why it is exceptionally difficult to calculate probabilities in the case of horse races, and yet people bet hundreds of millions of dollars on them. A little over a year ago, studying the possibilities of some formulas, I decided to look at some tip sheets, and subscribed to three. One of them was the *Track Almanac*, published by Cyril Orchard. Asked by the police why I chose that one, I could only say that I didn't know. I forget. That is suspicious, for them and you; for me, it is simply a fact that I don't remember. One day in February last year a daily double featured by Orchard came through, and I went to see him. He had some intelligence, and if he had been interested in the mathematical problems involved I could have made good use of him, but he wasn't. In spite of that I saw him occasionally, and he once spent a week end with me at the home of a friend in New Jersey. Altogether, previous to that broadcast, I had seen him, been with him, six times. That's suspicious, isn't it?"

"Moderately," Wolfe conceded.

Savarese nodded. "I'm glad to see you keep as objective as possible. But what about this? When I learned that a popular radio program on a national network had asked for opinions on the advisability of having a horse race tipster as a guest, I wrote a letter strongly urging it, asked for the privilege of being myself the second guest on the program, and suggested that Cyril Orchard should be the tipster invited."

Savarese smiled all over, beaming. "What about your one-in-five now?"

Wolfe grunted. "I didn't take that position. You assumed it for me. I suppose the police have that letter you wrote?"

"No, they haven't. No one has it. It seems that Miss Fraser's staff doesn't keep correspondence more than two or three weeks, and my letter has presumably been destroyed. If I had known that in time I might have been less candid in describing the letter's contents to the police, but on the other hand I might not have been. Obviously my treatment of that problem had an effect on my calculations of the probability of my being arrested for murder. But for a free decision I would have had to know, first, that the letter had been destroyed, and, second, that the memories of Miss Fraser's staff were vague about its contents. I learned both of those facts too late."

Wolfe stirred in his chair. "What else on the road to affirmative certainty?"

"Let's see." Savarese considered. "I think that's all, unless we go into observation of distributions, and that should be left for a secondary formula. For instance, my character, a study of which, *a posteriori*, would show it to be probable that I would commit murder for the sake of a sound but revolutionary formula. One detail of that would be my personal finances. My salary as an assistant professor is barely enough to live on endurably, but I paid ten dollars a week for that *Track Almanac*."

"Do you gamble? Do you bet on horse races?"

"No. I never have. I know too much—or rather, I know too little. More than ninety-nine per cent of the bets placed on horse races are outbursts of emotion, not exercises of reason. I restrict my emotions to the activities for which they are qualified." Savarese waved a hand. "That starts us in the other direction, toward a negative certainty, with its conclusion that I did not kill Orchard, and we might as well go on with it. Items:

"I could not have managed that Orchard got the poison. I was seated diagonally across from him, and I did not help pass the bottles. It cannot be shown that I have ever purchased, stolen, borrowed, or possessed any cyanide. It cannot be established that I would, did, or shall profit in any way from Orchard's death. When I arrived at the broadcasting studio, at twenty minutes to eleven, everyone else was already there and I would certainly have been observed if I had gone to the refrigerator and opened its door. There

45

is no evidence that my association with Orchard was other than as I have described it, with no element of animus or of any subjective attitude."

Savarese beamed. "How far have we gone? One-in-one-thousand?"

"I'm not with you," Wolfe said with no element of animus. "I'm not on that road at all, nor on any road. I'm wandering around poking at things. Have you ever been in Michigan?"

For the hour that was left before orchid time Wolfe fired questions at him, and Savarese answered him briefly and to the point. Evidently the professor really did want to compare Wolfe's technique with that of the police, for, as he gave close attention to each question as it was asked, he had more the air of a judge or referee sizing something up than of a murder suspect, guilty or innocent, going through an ordeal. The objective attitude.

He maintained it right up to four o'clock, when the session ended, and I escorted the objective attitude to the front door, and Wolfe went to his elevator.

A little after five Saul Panzer arrived. Coming only up to the middle of my ear, and of slight build, Saul doesn't even begin to fill the red leather chair, but he likes to sit in it, and did so. He is pretty objective too, and I have rarely seen him either elated or upset about anything that had happened to him, or that he had caused to happen to someone else, but that day he was really riled.

"It was bad judgment," he told me, frowning and glum. "Rotten judgment. I'm ashamed to face Mr. Wolfe. I had a good story ready, one that I fully expected to work, and all I needed was ten minutes with the mother to put it over. But I misjudged her. I had discussed her with a couple of the bellhops, and had talked with her on the phone, and had a good chance to size her up in the hotel lobby and when she came outside, and I utterly misjudged her. I can't tell you anything about her brains or character, I didn't get that far, but she certainly knows how to keep the dogs off. I came mighty close to spending the day in the pound."

He told me all about it, and I had to admit it was a gloomy tale. No operative likes to come away empty from as simple a job as that, and Saul Panzer sure doesn't. To get his mind off of it, I mixed him a highball and got out a deck of cards for a little congenial gin. When six o'clock came and brought Wolfe down from the plant rooms, ending the game, I had won something better than three bucks.

Saul made his report. Wolfe sat behind his desk and listened, without interruption or comment. At the end he told Saul he had nothing to apologize for, asked him to phone after dinner for instructions, and let him go. Left alone with me, Wolfe leaned back and shut his eyes and was not visibly even breathing. I got at my typewriter and tapped out a summary of Saul's report, and was on my way to the cabinet to file it when Wolfe's voice came:

"Archie."

"Yes, sir."

"I am stripped. This is no better than a treadmill."

"Yes, sir."

"I have to talk with that girl. Get Miss Fraser."

I did so, but we might as well have saved the nickel. Listening in on my phone, I swallowed it along with Wolfe. Miss Fraser was sorry that we had made little or no progress. She would do anything she could to help, but she was afraid, in fact she was certain, that it would be useless for her to call Mrs. Shepherd at Atlantic City and ask her to bring her daughter to New York to see Wolfe. There was no doubt that Mrs. Shepherd would flatly refuse. Miss Fraser admitted that she had influence with the child, Nancylee, but asserted that she had none at all with the mother. As for phoning Nancylee and persuading her to scoot and come on her own, she wouldn't consider it. She couldn't very well, since she had supplied the money for the mother and daughter to go away.

"You did?" Wolfe allowed himself to sound surprised. "Miss Koppel told Mr. Goodwin that none of you knew where they had gone."

"We didn't, until we saw it in the paper today. Nancylee's father was provoked, and that's putting it mildly, by all the photographers and reporters and everything else, and he blamed it on me, and I offered to pay the expense of a trip for them, but I didn't know where they decided to go."

We hung up, and discussed the outlook. I ventured to suggest two or three other possible lines of action, but Wolfe had his heart set on Nancylee, and I must admit I couldn't blame him for not wanting to start another round of conferences with the individuals he had been working on. Finally he said, in a tone that announced he was no longer discussing but telling me:

"I have to talk with that girl. Go and bring her."

I had known it was coming. "Conscious?" I asked casually.

"I said with her, not to her. She must be able to talk. You could revive her after you get her here. I should have sent you in the first place, knowing how you are with young women."

"Thank you very much. She's not a young woman, she's a minor. She wears socks."

"Archie."

"Yes, sir."

"Get her."

9

I HAD A bad break. An idea that came to me at the dinner table, while I was pretending to listen to Wolfe telling how men with mustaches a foot long used to teach mathematics in schools in Montenegro, required, if it was to bear fruit, some information from the janitor at 829 Wixley Avenue. But when, immediately after dinner, I drove up there, he had gone to the movies and I had to wait over an hour for him. I got what I hoped would be all I needed, generously ladled out another buck of Hi-Spot money, drove back downtown and put the car in the garage, and went home and up to my room. Wolfe, of course, was in the office, and the door was standing open, but I didn't even stop to nod as I went by.

In my room I gave my teeth an extra good brush, being uncertain how long they would have to wait for the next one, and then did my packing for the trip by putting a comb and hairbrush in my topcoat pocket. I didn't want to have a bag to take care of. Also I made a phone call. I made it there instead of in the office because Wolfe had put it off on me without a trace of a hint regarding ways and means, and if he wanted it like that okay. In that case there was no reason why he should listen to me giving careful and explicit instructions to Saul Panzer. Downstairs again, I did pause at the office door to tell him good night, but that was all I had for him.

Tuesday night I had had a little over three hours' sleep, and Wednesday night about the same. That night, Thursday, I had less than three, and only in snatches. At six-thirty Friday morning, when I emerged to the cab platform at the Atlantic City railroad station, it was still half dark, murky, chilly, and generally unattractive. I had me a good yawn, shivered from head to foot, told a taxi driver I was his customer but he would please wait for me a minute, and then stepped to the taxi just behind him and spoke to the driver of it:

"This time of day one taxi isn't enough for me, I always need two. I'll take the one in front and you follow, and when we stop we'll have a conference."

"Where you going?"

"Not far." I pushed a dollar bill at him. "You won't get lost."

He nodded without enthusiasm and kicked his starter. I climbed into the front cab and told the driver to pull up somewhere in the vicinity of the Ambassador Hotel. It wasn't much of a haul, and a few minutes later he rolled to the curb, which at that time of day had space to spare. When the other driver stopped right behind us I signaled to him, and he came and joined us.

"I have enemies," I told them.

They exchanged a glance and one of them said, "Work it out yourself, bud, we're just hackies. My meter says sixty cents."

"I don't mean that kind of enemies. It's wife and daughter. They're ruining my life. How many ways are there for people to leave the Ambassador Hotel? I don't mean dodges like fire escapes and coal chutes, just normal ways."

"Two," one said.

"Three," the other said.

"Make up your minds."

They agreed on three, and gave me the layout.

"Then there's enough of us," I decided. "Here." I shelled out two finifs, with an extra single for the one who had carried me to even them up. "The final payment will depend on how long it takes, but you won't have to sue me. Now listen."

They did so.

Ten minutes later, a little before seven, I was standing by some kind of a bush with no leaves on it, keeping an eye on the ocean-front entrance of the Ambassador. Gobs of dirty gray mist being batted around by icy gusts made it seem more like a last resort than a resort. Also I was realizing that I had made a serious mistake when I had postponed breakfast until there would be time to do it right. My stomach had decided that since it wasn't going to be needed any more it might as well try shriveling into a ball and see how I liked that. I tried to kid it along by swallowing, but because

49

I hadn't brushed my teeth it didn't taste like me at all, so I tried spitting instead, but that only made my stomach shrivel faster. After less than half an hour of it, when my watch said a quarter past seven, I was wishing to God I had done my planning better when one of my taxis came dashing around a corner to a stop, and the driver called to me and opened the door.

"They're off, bud."

"The station?"

"I guess so. That way." He made a U turn and stepped on the gas. "They came out the cab entrance and took one there. Tony's on their tail."

I didn't have to spur him on because he was already taking it hop, skip, and jump. My wrist watch told me nineteen past—eleven minutes before the seven-thirty for New York would leave. Only four of them had been used up when we did a fancy swerve and jerked to a stop in front of the railroad station. I hopped out. Just ahead of us a woman was paying her driver while a girl stood at her elbow.

"Duck, you damn fool," my driver growled at me. "They ain't blind, are they?"

"That's all right," I assured him. "They know I'm after them. It's a war of nerves."

Tony appeared from somewhere, and I separated myself from another pair of fives and then entered the station. There was only one ticket window working, and mother and child were at it, buying. I moseyed on to the train shed, still with three minutes to go, and was about to glance over my shoulder to see what was keeping them when they passed me on the run, holding hands, daughter in front and pulling Mom along. From the rear I saw them climb on board the train, but I stayed on the platform until the signal had been given and the wheels had started to turn, and then got on.

The diner wasn't crowded. I had a double orange juice, griddle cakes with broiled ham, coffee, French toast with sausage cakes, grape jelly, and more coffee. My stomach and I made up, and we agreed to forget it ever happened.

I decided to go have a look at the family, and here is something I'm not proud of. I had been so damn hungry that no thought of other stomachs had entered my head. But when, three cars back, I saw them and the look on their faces, the thought did come. Of course they were under other strains too, one in particular, but part of that pale, tight, anguished expression unquestionably came from hunger. They had had no time to grab anything on the way, and their manner of life was such that the idea of buying a meal on a train might not even occur to them.

I went back to the end of the car, stood facing the occupants, and called out:

"Get your breakfast in the dining car, three cars ahead! Moderate prices!"

Then I passed down the aisle, repeating it at suitable intervals, once right at their seat. It worked. They exchanged some words and then got up and staggered forward. Not only that, I had made other sales too: a woman, a man, and a couple.

By the time the family returned we were less than an hour from New York. I looked them over as they came down the aisle. Mother was small and round-shouldered and her hair was going gray. Her nose still looked thin and sharp-pointed, but not as much so as it had when she was starving. Nancylee was better-looking, and much more intelligent-looking, than I would have expected from her pictures in the papers or from Saul's description. She had lots of medium-brown hair coming below her shoulders, and blue eyes, so dark that you had to be fairly close to see the blue, that were always on the go. She showed no trace either of Mom's pointed nose or of Pop's acreage of brow. If I had been in high school I would gladly have bought her a Coke or even a sundae.

Danger would begin, I well knew, the minute they stepped off the train at Pennsylvania Station and mounted the stairs. I had decided what to do if they headed for a taxi or bus or the subway, or if Mom started to enter a phone booth. So I was right on their heels when the moment for action came, but the only action called for was a pleasant walk. They took the escalator to the street level, left the station by the north exit, and turned left. I trailed. At Ninth Avenue they turned uptown, and at Thirty-fifth Street left again. That cinched it that they were aiming straight for Wolfe's house, non-stop, and naturally I was anything but crestfallen, but what really did my heart good was the timing. It was exactly eleven o'clock, and Wolfe would get down from the plant rooms and settled in his chair just in time to welcome them.

So it was. West of Tenth Avenue they began looking at the numbers, and I began to close up. At our stoop they halted, took another look, and mounted the steps. By the time they were pushing the button I was at the bottom of the stoop, but they had taken no notice of me. It would have been more triumphant if I could have done it another way, but the trouble was that Fritz wouldn't let them in until he had checked with Wolfe. So I took the steps two at a time, used my key and flung the door open, and invited them:

"Mrs. Shepherd? Go right in."

She crossed the threshold. But Nancylee snapped at me:

"You were on the train. There's something funny about this."

"Mr. Wolfe's expecting you," I said, "if you want to call that funny. Anyway, come inside to laugh, so I can shut the door."

She entered, not taking her eyes off of me. I asked them if they wanted to leave their things in the hall, and they didn't, so I escorted them to the office. Wolfe, in his chair behind his desk, looked undecided for an instant and then got to his feet. I really appreciated that. He never rises when men enter, and his customary routine when a woman enters is to explain, if he feels like taking the trouble, that he keeps his chair because getting out of it and back in again is a more serious undertaking for him than for most men. I knew why he was breaking his rule. It was a salute to me, not just for producing them, but for getting them there exactly at the first minute of the day that he would be ready for them.

"Mrs. Shepherd," I said, "this is Mr. Nero Wolfe. Miss Nancylee Shepherd."

Wolfe bowed. "How do you do, ladies."

"My husband," Mom said in a scared but determined voice. "Where's my husband?"

"He'll be here soon," Wolfe assured her. "He was detained. Sit down, madam."

I grinned at him and shook my head. "Much obliged for trying to help, but that's not the line." I shifted the grin to the family. "I'll have to explain not only to you but to Mr. Wolfe too. Have you got the telegram with you? Let me have it a minute?"

Mom would have opened her handbag, but Nancylee stopped her. "Don't give it to him!" She snapped at me, "You let us out of here right now!"

"No," I said, "not right now, but I will in about five minutes if you still want to go. What are you afraid of? Didn't I see to it that you got some breakfast? First I would like to explain to Mr. Wolfe, and then I'll explain to you." I turned to Wolfe. "The telegram Mrs. Shepherd has in her bag reads as follows: *Take first train to New York and go to office of Nero Wolfe at 918 West Thirty-fifth Street. He is paying for this telegram. Bring Nan with you. Meet me there. Leave your things in your hotel room. Shake a leg. Al.* Saul sent it from a telegraph office in the Bronx at six-thirty this morning. You will understand why I had to go up there again to see the janitor. The *shake a leg* made it absolutely authentic, along with other things."

"Then Father didn't send it!" Nancylee was glaring at me. "I thought there was something funny about it!" She took her mother's arm. "Come on, we're going!"

"Where, Nan?"

"We're leaving here!"

"But where are we going?" Near-panic was in Mom's eyes and voice. "Home?"

"That's the point," I said emphatically. "That's just it. Where? You have three choices. First, you can go home and when the head of the family comes from work you can tell him how you were taken in by a fake telegram. Your faces show how much that appeals to you. Second, you can take the next train back to Atlantic City, but in that case I phone immediately, before you leave, to Mr. Shepherd at the warehouse where he works, and tell him that you're here with a wild tale about a telegram, and of course he'll want to speak to you. So again you would have to tell him about being fooled by a fake telegram."

Mom looked as if she needed some support, so I moved a chair up behind her and she sat.

"You're utterly awful," Nancylee said. "Just utterly!"

I ignored her and continued to her mother. "Or, third, you can stay here and Mr. Wolfe will discuss some matters with Nancylee, and ask her some questions. It may take two hours, or three, or four, so the sooner he gets started the better. You'll get an extra good lunch. As soon as Mr. Wolfe is through I'll take you to the station and put you on a train for Atlantic City. We'll pay your fare both ways and all expenses, such as taxi fare, and your breakfast, and dinner on the train going back. Mr. Shepherd, whom I have met, will never know anything about it." I screwed my lips. "Those are the only choices I can think of, those three."

Nancylee sat down and—another indication of her intelligence—in the red leather chair.

"This is terrible," Mom said hopelessly. "This is the worst

thing . . . you don't look like a man that would do a thing like this. Are you absolutely sure my husband didn't send that telegram? Honestly?"

"Positively not," I assured her. "He doesn't know a thing about it and never will. There's nothing terrible about it. Long before bedtime you'll be back in that wonderful hotel room."

She shook her head as if all was lost.

"It's not so wonderful," Nancylee asserted. "The shower squirts sideways and they won't fix it." Suddenly she clapped a hand to her mouth, went pop-eyed, and sprang from the chair.

"Jumping cats!" she squealed. "Where's your radio? It's Friday! She's broadcasting!"

"No radio," I said firmly. "It's out of order. Here, let me take your coat and hat."

10

DURING the entire performance, except when we knocked off for lunch, Mrs. Shepherd sat with sagging shoulders on one of the yellow chairs. Wolfe didn't like her there and at various points gave her suggestions, such as going up to the south room for a nap or up to the top to look at the orchids, but she wasn't moving. She was of course protecting her young, but I swear I think her main concern was that if she let us out of her sight we might pull another telegram on her signed Al.

I intend to be fair and just to Nancylee. It is quite true that this is on record, on a page of my notebook:

W: You have a high regard for Miss Fraser, haven't you, Miss Shepherd?

N: Oh, yes! She's simply utterly!

On another page:

W: Why did you leave high school without graduating if you were doing so well?

N: I was offered a modeling job. Just small time, two dollars an hour not very often and mostly legs, but the cash was simply sweet!

W: You're looking forward to a life of that—modeling?

N: Oh, no! I'm really very serious-minded. *Am* I! I'm going into radio. I'm going to have a program like Miss Fraser —you know, human and get the laughs, but worthwhile and *good*. How often have you been on the air, Mr. Wolfe?

On still another page:

W: How have you been passing your time at Atlantic City?

N: Rotting away. That place is as dead as last week's date. Simply stagnating. Utterly!

Those are verbatim, and there are plenty more where they came from, but there are other pages to balance them. She could talk to the point when she felt like it, as for instance when she explained that she would have been suspicious of the telegram, and would have insisted that her mother call her father at the warehouse by long distance, if she hadn't learned from the papers that Miss Fraser had engaged Nero Wolfe to work on the case. And when he got her going on the subject of Miss Fraser's staff, she not only showed that she had done a neat little job of sizing them up, but also conveyed it to us without including anything that she might be called upon either to prove or to eat.

It was easy to see how desperate Wolfe was from the way he confined himself, up to lunch time, to skating around the edges, getting her used to his voice and manner and to hearing him ask any and every kind of question. By the time Fritz summoned us to the dining room I couldn't see that he had got the faintest flicker of light from any direction.

When we were back in the office and settled again, with Mom in her same chair and Nancylee dragging on a cigarette as if she had been at it for years, Wolfe resumed as before, but soon I noticed that he was circling in toward the scene of the crime. After getting himself up to date on the East Bronx Fraser Girls' Club and how Nancylee had organized it and put it at the top, he went right on into the studio and began on the Fraser broadcasts. He leaned that Nancylee was always there on Tuesday, and sometimes on Friday too. Miss Fraser had promised her that she could get on a live mike some day, at least for a line or two. On the network! Most of the time she sat with the audience, front row, but she was always ready to help with anything, and frequently she was allowed to, but only on account of Miss Fraser. The others thought she was a nuisance.

"Are you?" Wolfe asked.

"You bet I am! But Miss Fraser doesn't think so because

55

she knows I think she's the very hottest thing on the air, simply super, and then there's my club, so you see how that is. The old ego mego."

You can see why I'd like to be fair and just to her.

Wolfe nodded as man to man. "What sort of things do you help with?"

"Oh." She waved a hand. "Somebody drops a page of script, I pick it up. One of the chairs squeaks, I hear it first and bring another one. The day it happened, I got the tray of glasses from the cabinet and took them to the table."

"You did? The day Mr. Orchard was a guest?"

"Sure, I often did that."

"Do you have a key to the cabinet?"

"No, Miss Vance has. She opened it and got the tray of glasses out." Nancylee smiled. "I broke one once, and did Miss Fraser throw a fit? No definitely. She just told me to bring a paper cup, that's how super she is."

"Marvelous. When did that happen?"

"Oh, a long while ago, when they were using the plain glasses, before they changed to the dark blue ones."

"How long ago was it?"

"Nearly a year, it must be." Nancylee nodded. "Yes, because it was when they first started to drink Hi-Spot on the program, and the first few times they used plain clear glasses and then they had to change—"

She stopped short.

"Why did they have to change?"

"I don't know."

I expected Wolfe to pounce, or at least to push. There was no doubt about it. Nancylee had stopped herself because she was saying, or starting to say, something that she didn't intend to let out, and when she said she didn't know she was lying. But Wolfe whirled and skated off:

"I suspect to get them so heavy they wouldn't break." He chuckled as if that were utterly amusing. "Have you ever drunk Hi-Spot, Miss Shepherd?"

"Me? Are you kidding? When my club got to the top they sent me ten cases. Truckloads!"

"I don't like it much. Do you?"

"Oh . . . I guess so. I guess I adore it, but not too much at a time. When I get my program and have Shepherd Clubs I'm going to work it a different way." She frowned. "Do you think Nancylee Shepherd is a good radio name, or is Nan Shepherd better, or should I make one up? Miss Fraser's name was Oxhall, and she married a man named Koppel but he died, and when she got into radio she didn't want to use either of them and made one up."

"Either of yours," Wolfe said judiciously, "would be excellent. You must tell me some time how you're going to handle your clubs. Do you think Hi-Spot has pepper in it?"

"I don't know, I never thought. It's a lot of junk mixed together. Not at all frizoo."

"No," Wolfe agreed, "not frizoo. What other things do you do to help out at the broadcasts?"

"Oh, just like I said."

"Do you ever help pass the glasses and bottles around—to Miss Fraser and Mr. Meadows and the guests?"

"No, I tried to once, but they wouldn't let me."

"Where were you—the day we're talking about—while that was being done?"

"Sitting on the piano bench. They want me to stay in the audience while they're on the air, but sometimes I don't."

"Did you see who did the passing—to Mr. Orchard, for instance?"

Nancylee smiled in good-fellowship. "Now you'd like to know that, wouldn't you? But I didn't. The police asked me that about twenty million times."

"No doubt. I ask you once. Do you ever take the bottles from the cabinet and put them in the refrigerator?"

"Sure, I often do that—or I should say I help. That's Miss Vance's job, and she can't carry them all at once, so she has to make two trips, so quite often she takes four bottles and I take three."

"I see. I shouldn't think she would consider you a nuisance. Did you help with the bottles that Tuesday?"

"No, because I was looking at the new hat Miss Fraser had on, and I didn't see Miss Vance starting to get the bottles."

"Then Miss Vance had to make two trips, first four bottles and then three?"

"Yes, because Miss Fraser's hat was really something for the preview. Utterly first run! It had—"

"I believe you." Wolfe's voice sharpened a little, though perhaps only to my experienced ear. "That's right, isn't it, first four bottles and then three?"

"Yes, that's right."

"Making a total of seven?"

"Oh, you can add!" Nancylee exclaimed delightedly. She

57

raised her right hand with four fingers extended, then her left hand with three, and looked from one to the other. "Correct. Seven!"

"Seven," Wolfe agreed. "I can add, and you can, but Miss Vance and Mr. Meadows can't. I understand that only four bottles are required for the program, but that they like to have extra ones in the refrigerator to provide for possible contingencies. But Miss Vance and Mr. Meadows say that the total is eight bottles. You say seven. Miss Vance says that they are taken from the cabinet to the refrigerator in two lots, four and four. You say four and three."

Wolfe leaned forward. "Miss Shepherd." His voice cut. "You will explain to me immediately, and satisfactorily, why they say eight and you say seven. Why?"

She didn't look delighted at all. She said nothing.

"Why?" It was the crack of a whip.

"I don't know!" she blurted.

I had both eyes on her, and even from a corner of one, with the other one shut, it would have been as plain as daylight that she did know, and furthermore that she had clammed and intended to stay clammed.

"Pfui." Wolfe wiggled a finger at her. "Apparently, Miss Shepherd, you have the crackbrained notion that whenever the fancy strikes you you can say you don't know, and I'll let it pass. You tried it about the glasses, and now this. I'll give you one minute to start telling me why the others said the customary number of bottles taken to the refrigerator is eight, and you say seven—Archie, time it."

I looked at my wrist, and then back at Nancylee. But she merely stayed a clam. Her face showed no sign that she was trying to make one up, or even figuring what would happen if she didn't. She was simply utterly not saying anything. I let her have an extra ten seconds, and then announced:

"It's up."

Wolfe sighed. "I'm afraid, Miss Shepherd, that you and your mother will not return to Atlantic City. Not today. It is—"

A sound of pain came from Mom—not a word, just a sound. Nancy cried:

"But you promised—"

"No. I did not. Mr. Goodwin did. You can have that out with him, but not until after I have given him some instructions." Wolfe turned to me. "Archie, you will escort Miss Shepherd to the office of Inspector Cramer. Her mother may accompany you or go home, as she prefers. But first take this down, type it, and take it with you. Two carbons. A letter to Inspector Cramer."

Wolfe leaned back, closed his eyes, pursed his lips, and in a moment began:

"Regarding the murder of Cyril Orchard, I send you this information by Mr. Goodwin, who is taking Miss Nancylee Shepherd to you. He will explain how Miss Shepherd was brought to New York from Atlantic City, Paragraph.

"I suggest that Miss Madeline Fraser should be arrested without delay, charged with the murder of Cyril Orchard. It is obvious that the members of her staff are joined in a conspiracy. At first I assumed that their purpose was to protect her, but I am now convinced that I was wrong. At my office Tuesday evening it was ludicrously transparent that they were all deeply concerned about Miss Fraser's getting home safely, or so I then thought. I now believe that their concern was of a very different kind. Paragraph.

"That evening, here, Mr. Meadows was unnecessarily explicit and explanatory when I asked him how he decided which bottles to take from the refrigerator. There were various other matters which aroused my suspicion, plainly pointing to Miss Fraser, among them their pretense that they cannot remember who placed the glass and bottle in front of Mr. Orchard, which is of course ridiculous. Certainly they remember; and it is not conceivable that they would conspire unanimously to defend one of their number from exposure, unless that one were Miss Fraser. They are moved, doubtless, by varying considerations—loyalty, affection, or merely the desire to keep their jobs, which they will no longer have after Miss Fraser is arrested and disgraced—and, I hope, punished as the law provides. Paragraph.

"All this was already in my mind, but not with enough conviction to put it to you thus strongly, so I waited until I could have a talk with Miss Shepherd. I have now done that. It is plain that she too is in the conspiracy, and that leaves no doubt that it is Miss Fraser who is being shielded from exposure, since Miss Shepherd would do anything for her but nothing for any of the others. Miss Shepherd has lied to me twice that I am sure of, once when she said that she didn't know why the glasses that they drank from were changed, and once when she would give no explanation of her contradiction of the others regarding the number of bottles put in the refrigerator. Mr. Goodwin will give you the details of that. Paragraph.

"When you have got Miss Fraser safely locked in a cell, I

59

would suggest that in questioning her you concentrate on the changing of the glasses. That happened nearly a year ago, and therefore it seems likely that the murder of Mr. Orchard was planned far in advance. This should make it easier for you, not harder, especially if you are able to persuade Miss Shepherd, by methods available to you, to tell all she knows about it. I do not—*Archie!*"

If Nancylee had had a split personality and it had been the gungirl half of her that suddenly sprang into action, I certainly would have been caught with my fountain pen down. But she didn't pull a gat. All she did was come out of her chair like a hurricane, get to me before I could even point the pen at her, snatch the notebook and hurl it across the room, and turn to blaze away at Wolfe:

"That's a lie! It's all a lie!"

"Now, Nan," came from Mrs. Shepherd, in a kind of shaky hopeless moan.

I was on my feet at the hurricane's elbow, feeling silly. Wolfe snapped at me:

"Get the notebook and we'll finish. She's hysterical. If she does it again put her in the bathroom."

Nancylee was gripping my coat sleeve. "No!" she cried. "You're a stinker, you know you are! Changing the glasses had nothing to do with it! And I don't know why they changed them either—you're just a stinker—"

"Stop it!" Wolfe commanded her. "Stop screaming. If you have anything to say, sit down and say it. Why did they change the glasses?"

"I don't know!"

In crossing the room for it I had to detour around Mom, and, doing so, I gave her a pat on the shoulder, but I doubt if she was aware of it. From her standpoint there was nothing left. When I got turned around Nancylee was still there, and from the stiffness of her back she looked put for the day. But as I reached my desk she spoke, no screaming:

"I honestly don't know why they changed the glasses, because I was just guessing but if I tell you what I was guessing I'll have to tell you something I promised Miss Fraser I would never tell anybody."

Wolfe nodded. "As I said. Shielding Miss Fraser."

"I'm not shielding her! She doesn't have to be shielded!"

"Don't get hysterical again. What was it you guessed?"

"I want to phone her."

"Of course you do. To warn her. So she can get away."

Nancylee slapped a palm on his desk.

"Don't do that!" he thundered.

"You're such a stinker!"

"Very well. Archie lock her in the bathroom and phone Mr. Cramer to send for her."

I stood up, but she paid no attention to me. "All right," she said, "then I'll tell her how you made me tell, and my mother can tell her, too. When they got the new glasses I didn't know why, but I noticed right away, the broadcast that day, about the bottles too. That day Miss Vance didn't take eight bottles, she only took seven. If it hadn't been for that I might not have noticed, but I did, and when they were broadcasting I saw that the bottle they gave Miss Fraser had a piece of tape on it. And every time after that it has always been seven bottles, and they always give Miss Fraser the one with tape on it. So I thought there was some connection, the new glasses and the tape on the bottle, but I was just guessing."

"I wish you'd sit down, Miss Shepherd. I don't like tipping my head back."

"I wouldn't care if you broke your old neck!"

"Now, Nan," her mother moaned.

Nancylee went to the red leather chair and lowered herself onto the edge of it.

"You said," Wolfe murmured, "that you promised Miss Fraser not to tell about this. When did you promise, recently?"

"No, a long time ago. Months ago. I was curious about the tape on the bottle, and one day I asked Miss Vance about it, and afterward Miss Fraser told me it was something very personal to her and she made me promise never to tell. Twice since then she has asked me if I was keeping the promise and I told her I was and I always would. And now here I am! But you saying she should be arrested for murder . . . just because I said I didn't know . . ."

"I gave other reasons."

"But she won't be arrested now, will she? The way I've explained?"

"We'll see. Probably not." Wolfe sounded comforting. "No one has ever told you what the tape is on the bottle for?"

"No."

"Haven't you guessed?"

"No, I haven't, and I'm not going to guess now. I don't

know what it's for or who puts it on or when they put it on, or anything about it except what I've said, that the bottle they give Miss Fraser has a piece of tape on it. And that's been going on a long time, nearly a year, so it couldn't have anything to do with that man getting murdered just last week. So I hope you're satisfied."

"Fairly well," Wolfe conceded.

"Then may I phone her now?"

"I'd rather you didn't. You see she has hired me to investigate this murder, and I'd prefer to tell her about this myself—and apologize for suspecting her. By the way, the day Mr. Orchard was poisoned—did Miss Fraser's bottle have tape on it that day as usual?"

"I didn't notice it that day, but I suppose so, it always did."

"You're sure you didn't notice it?"

"What do you think? Am I lying again?"

Wolfe shook his head. "I doubt it. You don't sound like it. But one thing you can tell me, about the tape. What was it like and where was it on the bottle?"

"Just a piece of Scotch tape, that's all, around the neck of the bottle, down nearly to where the bottle starts to get bigger."

"Always in the same place?"

"Yes."

"How wide is it?"

"You know, Scotch tape, about that wide." She held a thumb and fingertip about half an inch apart.

"What color?"

"Brown—or maybe it looks brown because the bottle is."

"Always the same color?"

"Yes."

"Then it couldn't have been very conspicuous."

"I didn't say it was conspicuous. It wasn't."

"You have good eyesight, of course, at your age." Wolfe glanced at the clock and turned to me. "When is the next train for Atlantic City?"

"Four-thirty," I told him.

"Then you have plenty of time. Give Mrs. Shepherd enough to cover all expenses. You will take her and her daughter to the station. Since they do not wish it to be known that they have made this trip, it would be unwise for them to do any telephoning, and of course you will make sure that they board the right train, and that the train actually starts. As you know, I do not trust trains either to start or, once started, to stop."

"We're going back," Mom said, unbelieving but daring to hope.

11

THERE was one little incident I shouldn't skip, on the train when I had found their seats for them and was turning to go. I had made no effort to be sociable, since their manner, especially Nancylee's, had made it plain that if I had stepped into a manhole they wouldn't even have halted to glance down in it. But as I turned to go Mom suddenly reached up to pat me on the shoulder. Apparently the pat I had given her at one of her darkest moments had been noticed after all, or maybe it was because I had got them Pullman seats. I grinned at her, but didn't risk offering to shake hands in farewell. I ride my luck only so far.

Naturally another party was indicated, but I didn't realize how urgent it was until I got back to the office and found a note, on a sheet from Wolfe's memo pad, waiting for me under a paperweight on my desk—he being, as per schedule, up in the plant rooms. The note said:

AG—
Have all seven of them here
at six o'clock.
NW

Just like snapping your fingers. I scowled at the note. Why couldn't it be after dinner, allowing more time both to get them and to work on them? Not to mention that I already had a fairly good production record for the day, with the 11:00 A.M. delivery I had made. My watch said ten to five. I swallowed an impulse to mount to the plant rooms and give him an argument, and reached for the phone.

I ran into various difficulties, including resistance to a summons on such short notice, with which I was in complete sympathy. Bill Meadows balked good, saying that he had already told Wolfe everything he knew, including the time he had thrown a baseball through a windowpane, and I had to put pressure on him with menacing hints. Madeline Fraser and Deborah Koppel were reluctant but had to admit that Wolfe should either be fired or given all possible help. They agreed to bring Elinor Vance. Nathan Traub, whom I got first, at his office, was the only one who offered no objection, though he commented that he would have to call off an important appointment. The only two I fell down on were Savarese and Strong. The professor had left town for the week end, I supposed to hunt formulas, and Tully Strong just couldn't be found, though I tried everywhere, including all the sponsors.

Shortly before six I phoned up to Wolfe to report. The best he had for me was a grunt. I remarked that five out of seven, at that hour on a Friday, was nothing to be sneezed at. He replied that seven would have been better.

"Yeah," I agreed. "I've sent Savarese and Strong telegrams signed Al, but what if they don't get them on time?"

So there were five. Wolfe doesn't like to be seen, by anyone but Fritz or me sitting around waiting for people, I imagine on the theory that it's bad for his prestige, and therefore he didn't come down to the office until I passed him the word that all five were there. Then he favored us by appearing. He entered, bowed to them, crossed to his chair, and got himself comfortable. It was cozier and more intimate than it had been three days earlier, with the gate-crashers absent.

There was a little conversation. Traub offered some pointed remarks about Wolfe's refusal to admit reporters for an interview. Ordinarily, with an opening like that, Wolfe counters with a nasty crusher, but now he couldn't be bothered. He merely waved it away.

"I got you people down here," he said, perfectly friendly, "for a single purpose, and if you're not to be late for your dinners we'd better get at it. Tuesday evening I told you that you are all lying to me, but I didn't know then how barefaced you were about it. Why the devil didn't you tell me about the piece of tape on Miss Fraser's bottle?"

They all muffed it badly, even Miss Fraser, with the sole exception of Traub. He alone looked just bewildered.

"Tape?" he asked. "What tape?"

It took the other four an average of three seconds even to begin deciding what to do about their faces.

"Who is going to tell me about it?" Wolfe inquired. "Not all of you at once. Which one?"

"But," Bill Meadows stammered, "we don't know what you're talking about."

"Nonsense." Wolfe was less friendly. "Don't waste time on that. Miss Shepherd spent most of the day here and I know all about it." His eyes stopped on Miss Fraser. "She couldn't help it, madam. She did quite well for a child, and she surrendered only under the threat of imminent peril to you."

"What's this all about?" Traub demanded.

"It's nothing, Nat," Miss Fraser assured him. "Nothing of any importance. Just a little . . . a sort of joke . . . among us . . . that you don't know about. . . ."

"Nothing to it!" Bill Meadows said, a little too loud. "There's a perfectly simple—"

"Wait, Bill." Deborah Koppel's voice held quiet authority. Her gaze was at Wolfe. "Will you tell us exactly what Nancylee said?"

"Certainly," Wolfe assented. "The bottle served to Miss Fraser on the broadcast is always identified with a strip of Scotch tape. That has been going on for months, nearly a year. The tape is either brown, the color of the bottle, or transparent, is half an inch wide, and encircles the neck of the bottle near the shoulder."

"Is that all she told you?"

"That's the main thing. Let's get that explained. What's the tape for?"

"Didn't Nancylee tell you?"

"She said she didn't know."

Deborah was frowning. "Why she must know! It's quite simple. As we told you, when we get to the studio the day of a broadcast Miss Vance takes the bottles from the cabinet and puts them in the refrigerator. But that gives them only half an hour or a little longer to get cold, and Miss Fraser likes hers as cold as possible, so a bottle for her is put in earlier and the tape put on to tell it from the others."

"Who puts it there and when?"

"Well—that depends. Sometimes one of us puts it there the day before . . . sometimes it's one left over from the preceding broadcast. . . ."

"Good heavens," Wolfe murmured. "I didn't know you were an imbecile, Miss Koppel."

"I am not an imbecile, Mr. Wolfe."

"I'll have to have more than your word for it. I presume the explanation you have given me was concocted to satisfy the casual curiosity of anyone who might notice the tape on the bottle—and, incidentally, I wouldn't be surprised if it was offered to Miss Shepherd and after further observation she rejected it. That's one thing she didn't tell me. For that purpose the explanation would be adequate—except with Miss Shepherd—but to try it on me! I'll withdraw the 'imbecile,' since I blurted it at you without warning, but I do think you might have managed something a little less flimsy."

"It may be flimsy," Bill Meadows put in aggressively, "but it happens to be true."

"My dear sir." Wolfe was disgusted. "You too? Then why didn't it satisfy Miss Shepherd, if it was tried on her, and why was she sworn to secrecy? Why weren't all the bottles put in the refrigerator in advance, to get them all cold, instead of just the one for Miss Fraser? There are—"

"Because someone—" Bill stopped short.

"Precisely," Wolfe agreed with what he had cut off. "Because hundreds of people use that studio between Miss Fraser's broadcasts, and someone would have taken them from the refrigerator, which isn't locked. That's what you were about to say, but didn't, because you realized there would be the same hazard for one bottle as for eight." Wolfe shook his head. "No, it's no good. I'm tired of your lies; I want the truth; and I'll get it because nothing else can meet the tests I am now equipped to apply. Why is the tape put on the bottle?"

They looked at one another.

"No," Deborah Koppel said to anybody and everybody.

"What *is* all this?" Traub demanded peevishly.

No one paid any attention to him.

"Why not," Wolfe inquired, "try me with the same answer you have given the police?"

No reply.

Elinor Vance spoke, not to Wolfe. "It's up to you, Miss Fraser. I think we have to tell him."

"No," Miss Koppel insisted.

"I don't see any other way out of it, Debby," Madeline Fraser declared. "You shouldn't have told him that silly lie. It wasn't good enough for him and you know it." Her gray-green eyes went to Wolfe. "It would be fatal for me, for all of us, if this became known. I don't suppose you would give me your word to keep it secret?"

"How could I, madam?" Wolfe turned a palm up. "Under the circumstances? But I'll share it as reluctantly, and as narrowly, as the circumstances will permit."

"All right. Damn that Cyril Orchard, for making this necessary. The tape on the bottle shows that it is for me. My bottle doesn't contain Hi-Spot. I can't drink Hi-Spot."

"Why not?"

"It gives me indigestion."

"Good God!" Nathan Traub cried, his smooth low-pitched voice transformed into a squeak.

"I can't help it, Nat," Miss Fraser told him firmly, "but it does."

"And that," Wolfe demanded, "is your desperate and fatal secret?"

She nodded. "My Lord, could anything be worse? If that got around? If Leonard Lyons got it, for instance? I stuck to it the first few times, but it was no use. I wanted to cut that from the program, serving it, but by that time the Hi-Spot people were crazy about it, especially Anderson and Owen, and of course I couldn't tell them the truth. I tried faking it, not drinking much, but even a few sips made me sick. It must be an allergy."

"I congratulate you," Wolfe said emphatically.

"Good God," Traub muttered. He pointed a finger at Wolfe. "It is absolutely essential that this get to no one. No one whatever!"

"It's out now," Miss Koppel said quietly but tensely. "It's gone now."

"So," Wolfe asked, "you used a substitute?"

"Yes." Miss Fraser went on: "It was the only way out. We used black coffee. I drink gallons of it anyhow, and I like it either hot or cold. With sugar in it. It looks enough like Hi-Spot, which is dark brown, and of course in the bottle it can't be seen anyway, and we changed to dark blue glasses so it couldn't be seen that it didn't fizz."

"Who makes the coffee?"

"My cook, in my apartment."

"Who bottles it?"

"She does—my cook—she puts it in a Hi-Spot bottle, and puts the cap on."

"When, the day of the broadcast?"

"No, because it would still be hot, or at least warm, so she does it the day before and puts it in the refrigerator."

"Not at the broadcasting studio?"

"Oh, no, in my kitchen."

"Does she put the tape on it?"

"No, Miss Vance does that. In the morning she gets it— she always comes to my apartment to go downtown with me—and she puts the tape on it, and takes it to the studio in her bag, and puts it in the refrigerator there. She has to be careful not to let anyone see her do that."

"I feel better," Bill Meadows announced abruptly. He had his handkerchief out and was wiping his forehead.

"Why?" Wolfe asked him.

"Because I knew this had to come sooner or later, and I'm glad it was you that got it instead of the cops. It's been a cockeyed farce, all this digging to find out who had it in for this guy Orchard. Nobody wanted to poison Orchard. The poison was in the coffee and Orchard got it by mistake."

That finished Traub. A groan came from him, his chin went down, and he sat shaking his head in despair.

Wolfe was frowning. "Are you trying to tell me that the police don't know that the poisoned bottle held coffee?"

"Oh, sure, they know that." Bill wanted to help now. "But they've kept it under their hats. You notice it hasn't been in the papers. And none of us has spilled it, you can see why we wouldn't. They know it was coffee all right, but they think it was meant for Orchard, and it wasn't, it was meant for Miss Fraser."

Bill leaned forward and was very earnest. "Damn it, don't you see what we're up against? If we tell it and it gets known, God help the program! We'd get hooted off the air. But as long as we don't tell it, everybody thinks the poison was meant for Orchard, and that's why I said it was a farce. Well, we didn't tell, and as far as I'm concerned we never would."

"How have you explained the coffee to the police?"

"We haven't explained it. We didn't know how the poison got in the bottle, did we? Well, we didn't know how the coffee got there either. What else could we say?"

"Nothing, I suppose, since you blackballed the truth. How have you explained the tape?"

"We haven't explained it."

"Why not?"

"We haven't been asked to."

"Nonsense. Certainly you have."

"I haven't."

"Thanks, Bill." It was Madeline Fraser, smiling at him. "But there's no use trying to save any pieces." She turned to Wolfe. "He's trying to protect me from—don't they call it tampering with evidence? You remember that after the doctor came Mr. Strong took the four bottles from the table and started off with them, just a foolish impulse he had,

68

and Mr. Traub and I took them from him and put them back on the table."

Wolfe nodded.

"Well, that was when I removed the tape from the bottle."

"I see. Good heavens! It's a wonder all of you didn't collectively gather them up, and the glasses, and march to the nearest sink to wash up." Wolfe went back to Bill. "You said Mr. Orchard got the poisoned coffee by mistake. How did that happen?"

"Traub gave it to him. Traub didn't—"

Protests came at him from both directions, all of them joining in. Traub even left his chair to make it emphatic.

Bill got a little flushed, but he was stubborn and heedless. "Since we're telling it," he insisted, "we'd better tell it all."

"You're not sure it was Nat," Miss Koppel said firmly.

"Certainly I'm sure! You know damn well it was! You know damn well we all saw—all except Lina—that Orchard had her bottle, and of course it was Traub that gave it to him, because Traub was the only one that didn't know about the tape. Anyhow I saw him!—That's the way it was, Mr. Wolfe. But when the cops started on us apparently we all had the same idea—I forget who started it—that it would be best not to remember who put the bottle in front of Orchard. So we didn't. Now that you know about the tape, I do remember, and if the others don't they ought to."

"Quit trying to protect me, Bill," Miss Fraser scolded him. "It was my idea, about not remembering. I started it."

Again several of them spoke at once. Wolfe showed them a palm:

"Please!—Mr. Traub. Manifestly it doesn't matter whether you give me a yes or a no, since you alone were not aware that one of the bottles had a distinction; but I ask you pro forma, did you place that bottle before Mr. Orchard?"

"I don't know," Traub said belligerently, "and I don't care. Meadows doesn't know either."

"But you did help pass the glasses and bottles around?"

"I've told you I did. I thought it was fun." He threw up both hands. "Fun!"

"There's one thing," Madeline Fraser put in, for Wolfe. "Mr. Meadows said that they all saw that Mr. Orchard had my bottle, except me. That's only partly true. I didn't notice it at first, but when I lifted the glass to drink and smelled the Hi-Spot I knew someone else had my glass. I went ahead and faked the drinking, and as I went on with the script I saw that the bottle with the tape on it was a littler nearer to him than to me—as you know, he sat across from me. I had to decide quick what to do—not me with the Hi-Spot, but him with the coffee. I was afraid he would blurt out that it tasted like coffee, especially since he had taken two big gulps. I was feeling relieved that apparently he wasn't going to, when he sprang up with that terrible cry . . . so what Mr. Meadows said was only partly true. I suppose he was protecting me some more, but I'm tired of being protected by everybody."

"He isn't listening, Lina," Miss Koppel remarked.

It was a permissible conclusion, but not necessarily sound. Wolfe had leaned back in his chair and closed his eyes, and even to me it might have seemed that he was settling for a snooze but for two details: first, dinner time was getting close, and second, the tip of his right forefinger was doing a little circle on the arm of his chair, around and around. The silence held for seconds, made a minute, and started on another one.

Someone said something.

Wolfe's eyes came half open and he straightened up.

"I could," he said, either to himself or to them, "ask you to stay to dinner. Or to return after dinner. But if Miss Fraser is tired of being protected, I am tired of being hum-bugged. There are things I need to know, but I don't intend to try to pry them out of you without a lever. If you are ready to let me have them, I'm ready to take them. You know what they are as well as I do. It now seems obvious that this was an attempt to kill Miss Fraser. What further evidence is there to support that assumption, and what evidence is there, if any, to contradict it? Who wants Miss Fraser to die, and why? Particularly, who of those who had access to the bottle of coffee, at any time from the moment it was bottled at her apartment to the moment when it was served at the broadcast? And so on. I won't put all the questions; you know what I want. Will any of you give it to me—any of it?"

His gaze passed along the line. No one said a word.

"One or more of you," he said, "might prefer not to speak in the presence of the others. If so, do you want to come back later? This evening?"

"If I had anything to tell you," Bill Meadows asserted, "I'd tell you now."

"You sure would," Traub agreed.

"I thought not," Wolfe said grimly. "To get anything out

of you another Miss Shepherd would be necessary. One other chance: if you prefer not even to make an appointment in the presence of the others, we are always here to answer the phone. But I would advise you not to delay." He pushed his chair back and got erect. "That's all I have for you now, and you have nothing for me."

They didn't like that much. They wanted to know what he was going to do. Especially and unanimously, they wanted to know what about their secret. Was the world going to hear of what a sip of Hi-Spot did to Madeline Fraser? On that Wolfe refused to commit himself. The stubbornest of the bunch was Traub. When the others finally left he stayed behind, refusing to give up the fight, even trying to follow Wolfe into the kitchen. I had to get rude to get rid of him.

When Wolfe emerged from the kitchen, instead of bearing left toward the dining room he returned to the office, although dinner was ready.

I followed. "What's the idea? Not hungry?"

"Get Mr. Cramer."

I went to my desk and obeyed.

Wolfe got on.

"How do you do, sir." He was polite but far from servile. "Yes. No. No, indeed. If you will come to my office after dinner, say at nine o'clock, I'll tell you why you haven't got anywhere on that Orchard case. No, not only that, I think you'll find it helpful. No, nine o'clock would be better."

He hung up, scowled at me, and headed for the dining room. By the time he had seated himself, tucked his napkin in the V of his vest, and removed the lid from the onion soup, letting the beautiful strong steam sail out, his face had completely cleared and he was ready to purr.

12

INSPECTOR CRAMER, adjusted to ease in the red leather chair, with beer on the little table at his elbow, manipulated his jaw so that the unlighted cigar made a cocky upward angle from the left side of his mouth.

"Yes," he admitted. "You can have it all for a nickel. That's where I am. Either I'm getting older or murderers are getting smarter."

He was in fact getting fairly gray and his middle, though it would never get into Wolfe's class, was beginning to make pretensions, but his eyes were as sharp as ever and his heavy broad shoulders showed no inclination to sink under the load.

"But," he went on, sounding more truculent than he actually was because keeping the cigar where he wanted it made him talk through his teeth, "I'm not expecting any nickel from you. You don't look as if you needed anything. You look as pleased as if someone had just given you a geranium."

"I don't like geraniums."

"Then what's all the happiness about? Have you got to the point where you're ready to tell Archie to mail out the bills?"

He not only wasn't truculent; he was positively mushy. Usually he called me Goodwin. He called me Archie only when he wanted to peddle the impression that he regarded himself as one of the family, which he wasn't.

Wolfe shook his head. "No, I'm far short of that. But I am indeed pleased. I like the position I'm in. It seems likely that you and your trained men—up to a thousand of them, I assume, on a case as blazoned as this one—are about to work like the devil to help me earn a fee. Isn't that enough to give me a smirk?"

"The hell you say." Cramer wasn't so sugary. "According to the papers your fee is contingent."

"So it is."

"On what you do. Not on what we do."

"Of course," Wolfe agreed. He leaned back and sighed comfortably. "You're much too clearsighted not to appraise the situation, which is a little peculiar, as I do. Would you like me to describe it?"

"I'd love it. You're a good describer."

"Yes, I think I am. You have made no progress, and after ten days you are sunk in a morass, because there is a cardinal fact which you have not discovered. I have. I have discovered it by talking with the very persons who had been questioned by you and your men many times, and it was not given to me willingly. Only by intense and sustained effort did I dig it out. Then why should I pass it on to you? Why don't I use it myself, and go on to triumph?"

Cramer put his beer glass down. "You're telling me."

"That was rhetoric. The trouble is that, while without this fact you can't even get started, with it there is still a job to be done; that job will require further extended dealing with these same people, their histories and relationships; and I have gone as far as I can with them unless I hire an army. You already have an army. The job will probably need an enormous amount of the sort of work for which your men are passably equipped, some of them even adequately, so why shouldn't they do it? Isn't it the responsibility of the police to catch a murderer?"

Cramer was now wary and watchful. "From you," he said, "that's one hell of a question. More rhetoric?"

"Oh, no. That one deserves an answer. Yours, I feel sure, is yes, and the newspapers agree. So I submit a proposal: I'll give you the fact, and you'll proceed to catch the murderer. When that has been done, you and I will discuss whether the fact was essential to your success; whether you could possibly have got the truth and the evidence without it. If we agree that you couldn't, you will so inform my clients, and I shall collect my fee. No document will be required; an oral statement will do; and of course only to my clients. I don't care what you say to journalists or to your superior officers."

Cramer grunted. He removed the cigar from his mouth, gazed at the mangled end suspiciously as if he expected to see a bug crawling, and put it back where it belonged. Then he squinted at Wolfe:

"Would you repeat that?"

Wolfe did so, as if he were reading it off, without changing a word.

Cramer grunted again. "You say if we agree. You mean if you agree with me, or if I agree with you?"

"Bah. It couldn't be plainer."

"Yeah. When you're plainest you need looking at closest. What if I've already got this wonderful fact?"

"You didn't have it two hours ago. If you have it now, I have nothing to give and shall get nothing. If when I divulge it you claim to have had it, you'll tell me when and from whom you got it." Wolfe stirred impatiently. "It is, of course, connected with facts in your possession—for instance, that the bottle contained sugared coffee instead of Hi-Spot."

"Sure, they've told you that."

"Or that your laboratory has found traces of a certain substance, in a band half an inch wide, encircling the neck of the bottle."

"They haven't told you *that*." Cramer's eyes got narrower. "There are only six or seven people who could have told you that, and they all get paid by the City of New York, and by God you can name him before we go any farther."

"Pfui." Wolfe was disgusted. "I have better use for my clients' money than buying information from policemen. Why don't you like my proposal? What's wrong with it? Frankly, I hope to heaven you accept it, and immediately. If you don't I'll have to hire two dozen men and begin all over again on those people, and I'd rather eat baker's bread —almost."

"All right." Cramer did not relax. "Hell, I'd do anything to save you from that. I'm on. Your proposal, as you have twice stated it, provided I get the fact, and all of it, here and now."

"You do. Here it is, and Mr. Goodwin will have a typed copy for you. But first—a little detail—I owe it to one of my clients to request that one item of it be kept confidential, if it can possibly be managed."

"I can't keep murder evidence confidential."

"I know you can't. I said if it can possibly be managed."

"I'll see, but I'm not promising, and if I did promise I probably wouldn't keep it. What's the item? Give it to me first."

"Certainly. Miss Fraser can't drink Hi-Spot because it gives her indigestion."

"What the hell." Cramer goggled at him. "Orchard didn't drink Hi-Spot, he drank coffee, and it didn't give him indigestion, it killed him."

Wolfe nodded. "I know. But that's the item, and on behalf of my clients I ask that it be kept undisclosed if possible. This is going to take some time, perhaps an hour, and your glass and bottle are empty. Archie?"

I got up and bartended without any boyish enthusiasm because I wasn't very crazy about the shape things were taking. I was keeping my fingers crossed. If Wolfe was starting some tricky maneuver and only fed him a couple of crumbs, with the idea of getting a full-sized loaf, not baker's bread, in exchange, that would be one thing, and I was ready to applaud if he got away with it. If he really opened the bag and dumped it out, letting Cramer help himself, that would be something quite different. In that case he was playing it straight, and that could only mean that he had got fed up with them, and really intended to sit and read poetry or draw horses and let the cops earn his fee for him. That did not appeal to me. Money may be everything, but it makes a difference how you get it.

He opened the bag and dumped it. He gave Cramer all we had. He even quoted, from memory, the telegram that had been sent to Mom Shepherd, and as he did so I had to clamp my jaw to keep from making one of four or five remarks that would have fitted the occasion. I had composed that telegram, not him. But I kept my trap shut. I do sometimes ride him in the presence of outsiders, but rarely for Cramer to hear, and not when my feelings are as strong as they were then.

Also Cramer had a lot of questions to ask, and Wolfe answered them like a lamb. And I had to leave my chair so Cramer could rest his broad bottom on it while he phoned his office.

"Rowcliff? Take this down, but don't broadcast it." He was very crisp and executive, every inch an inspector. "I'm at Wolfe's office, and he did have something, and for once I think he's dealing off the top of the deck. We've got to start all over. It's one of those goddam babies where the wrong person got killed. It was intended for the Fraser woman. I'll tell you when I get there, in half an hour, maybe a little more. Call in everybody that's on the case. Find out where the Commissioner is, and the D.A. Get that Elinor Vance and that Nathan Traub, and get the cook at the Fraser apartment. Have those three there by the time I come. We'll take the others in the morning. Who was it went to Michigan—oh, I remember, Darst. Be sure you don't miss him, I want to see him. . . ."

And so forth. After another dozen or so executive orders Cramer hung up and returned to the red leather chair.

"What else?" he demanded.

"That's all," Wolfe declared. "I wish you luck."

Having dropped his chewed-up cigar in my wastebasket when he usurped my chair, Cramer got out another one and stuck it in his mouth without looking at it. "I'll tell you," he said. "You gave me a fact, no doubt about that, but this is the first time I ever saw you turn out all your pockets, so I sit down again. Before I leave I'd like to sit here a couple of minutes and ask myself, what for?"

Wolfe chuckled. "Didn't I just hear you telling your men to start to work for me?"

"Yeah, I guess so." The cigar slanted up. "It seems plausible, but I've known you to seem plausible before. And I swear to God if there's a gag in this it's buried too deep for me. You don't even make any suggestions."

"I have none."

And he didn't. I saw that. And there wasn't any gag. I didn't wonder that Cramer suspected him, considering what his experiences with him had been in the past years, but to me it was only too evident that Wolfe had really done a strip act, to avoid overworking his brain. I have sat in that office with him too many hours, and watched him put on his acts for too many audiences, not to know when he is getting up a charade. I certainly don't always know what he is up to, but I do know when he is up to nothing at all. He was simply utterly going to let the city employees do it.

"Would you suggest, for instance," Cramer inquired, "to haul Miss Fraser in on a charge of tampering with evidence? Or the others for obstructing justice?"

Wolfe shook his head. "My dear sir, you are after a murderer, not tamperers or obstructers. Anyway you can't get convictions on charges like that, except in very special cases, and you know it. You are hinting that it isn't like me to expose a client to such a charge, but will you arrest her? No. What you will do, I hope, is find out who it is that wants to kill her. How could I have suggestions for you? You know vastly more about it than I do. There are a thousand lines of investigation, in a case like this, on which I haven't moved a finger; and doubtless you have explored all of them. I won't insult you by offering a list of them. I'll be here, though, I'm always here, should you want a word with me."

Cramer got up and went.

13

I CAN'T deny that from a purely practical point of view the deal that Wolfe made with Cramer that Friday evening was slick, even fancy, and well designed to save wear and tear on Wolfe's energy and the contents of his skull. No matter how it added up at the end it didn't need one of Professor Savarese's formulas to show how probable it was that the fact Wolfe had furnished Cramer would turn out to be an essential item. That was a good bet at almost any odds.

But.

There was one fatal flaw in the deal. The city scientists, in order to earn Wolfe's fee for him while he played around with his toys, had to crack the case. That was the joker. I have never seen a more completely uncracked case than that one was, a full week after Wolfe had made his cute little arrangement to have his detective work done by proxy. I kept up to date on it both by reading the newspapers and by making jaunts down to Homicide headquarters on Twentieth Street, for chats with Sergeant Purley Stebbins or other acquaintances, and twice with Cramer himself. That was humiliating, but I did want to keep myself informed somehow about the case Wolfe and I were working on. For the first time in history I was perfectly welcome at Homicide, especially after three or four days had passed. It got to be pathetic, the way they would greet me like a treasured pal, no doubt thinking it was just possible I had come to contribute another fact. God knows they needed one. For of course they were reading the papers too, and the press was living up to one of its oldest traditions by bawling hell out of the cops for bungling a case which, by prompt and competent —you know how it goes.

So far the public had not been informed that Hi-Spot gave Miss Fraser indigestion. If the papers had known that!

Wolfe wasn't lifting a finger. It was not, properly speaking, a relapse. Relapse is my word for it when he gets so offended or disgusted by something about a case, or so appalled by the kind or amount of work it is going to take to solve it, that he decides to pretend he has never heard of it, and rejects it as a topic of conversation. This wasn't like that. He just didn't intend to work unless he had to. He was perfectly willing to read the pieces in the papers, or to put down his book and listen when I returned from one of my visits to Homicide. But if I tried to badger him into some mild exertion like hiring Saul and Fred and Orrie to look under some stones, or even thinking up a little errand for me, he merely picked up his book again.

If any of the developments, such as they were, meant anything to him, he gave no sign of it. Elinor Vance was arrested, held as a material witness, and after two days released on bail. The word I brought from Homicide was that there was nothing to it except that she had by far the best opportunity to put something in the coffee, with the exception of the cook. Not that there weren't plenty of others; the list had been considerably lengthened by the discovery that the coffee had been made, bottled, and kept overnight in Miss Fraser's apartment, with all the coming and going there.

Then there was the motive-collecting operation. In a murder case you can always get some motives together, but the trouble is you can never be sure which ones are sunfast for the people concerned. It all depends. There was the guy in Brooklyn a few years ago who stabbed a dentist in and around the heart eleven times because he had pulled the wrong tooth. In this case the motive assortment was about average, nothing outstanding but fairly good specimens. Six months ago Miss Fraser and Bill Meadows had had a first-class row, and she had fired him and he had been off the program for three weeks. They both claimed that they now dearly loved each other.

Not long ago Nat Traub had tried to persuade a soup manufacturer, one of the Fraser sponsors, to leave her and sign up for an evening comedy show, and Miss Fraser had retaliated by talking the sponsor into switching to another agency. Not only that, there were vague hints that Miss Fraser had started a campaign for a similar switch by other sponsors, including Hi-Spot, but they couldn't be nailed down. Again, she and Traub insisted that they were awful good friends.

The Radio Writers Guild should have been delighted to poison Miss Fraser on account of her tough attitude toward demands of the Guild for changes in contracts, and Elinor Vance was a member of the Guild in good standing. As for Tully Strong, Miss Fraser had opposed the formation of a Sponsors' Council, and still didn't like it, and of course if the were no Council there would be no secretary.

And so on. As motives go, worth tacking up but not spectacular. The one that would probably have got the popular vote was Deborah Koppel's. Somebody in the D.A.'s office had induced Miss Fraser to reveal the contents of her will. It left ten grand each to a niece and nephew, children of her sister who lived in Michigan, and all the rest to Deborah. It would be a very decent chunk, somewhere in six figures, with the first figure either a 2 or a 3, certainly worth a little investment in poison for anyone whose mind ran in that direction. There was, however, not the slightest indication that Deborah's mind did. She and Miss Fraser, then Miss Oxhall,

78

had been girlhood friends in Michigan, had taught at the same school, and had become sisters-in-law when Madeline had married Deborah's brother Lawrence.

Speaking of Lawrence, his death had of course been looked into again, chiefly on account of the coincidence of the cyanide. He had been a photographer and therefore, when needing cyanide, all he had to do was reach to a shelf for it. What if he hadn't killed himself after all? Or what if, even if he had, someone thought he hadn't, believed it was his wife who had needed the cyanide in order to collect five thousand dollars in insurance money, and had now arranged, after six years, to even up by giving Miss Fraser a dose of it herself?

Naturally the best candidate for that was Deborah Koppel. But they couldn't find one measly scrap to start a foundation with. There wasn't the slightest evidence, ancient or recent, that Deborah and Madeline had ever been anything but devoted friends, bound together by mutual interest, respect, and affection. Not only that, the Michigan people refused to bat an eye at the suggestion that Lawrence Koppel's death had not been suicide. He had been a neurotic hypochondriac, and the letter he had sent to his best friend, a local lawyer, had cinched it. Michigan had been perfectly willing to answer New York's questions, but for themselves they weren't interested.

Another of the thousand lines that petered out into nothing was the effort to link up one of the staff, especially Elinor Vance, with Michigan. They had tried it before with Cyril Orchard, and now they tried it with the others. No soap. None of them had ever been there.

Wolfe, as I say, read some of this in the papers, and courteously listened to the rest of it, and much more, from me. He was not, however, permitted to limit himself strictly to the role of spectator. Cramer came to our office twice during that week, and Anderson, the Hi-Spot president, once; and there were others.

There was Tully Strong, who arrived Saturday afternoon, after a six-hour session with Cramer and an assortment of his trained men. He had probably been pecked at a good deal, as all of them had, since they had told the cops a string of barefaced lies, and he was not in good humor. He was so sore that when he put his hands on Wolfe's desk and leaned over at him to make some remarks about treachery, and his spectacles slipped forward nearly to the tip of his nose, he didn't bother to push them back in place.

His theory was that the agreement with Wolfe was null and void because Wolfe had violated it. Whatever happened, Wolfe not only would not collect his fee, he would not even be reimbursed for expenses. Moreover, he would be sued for damages. His disclosure of a fact which, if made public, would inflict great inquiry on Miss Fraser and her program, the network, and Hi-Spot, was irresponsible and inexcusable, and certainly actionable.

Wolfe told him bosh, he had not violated the agreement.

"No?" Strong straightened up. His necktie was to one side and his hair needed a comb and brush. His hand went up to his spectacles, which were barely hanging on, but instead of pushing them back he removed them. "You think not? You'll see. And, besides, you have put Miss Fraser's life in danger! I was trying to protect her! We all were!"

"All?" Wolfe objected. "Not all. All but one."

"Yes, all!" Strong had come there to be mad and would have no interference. "No one knew, no one but us, that it was meant for her! Now everybody knows it! Who can protect her now? I'll try, we all will, but what chance have we got?"

It seemed to me he was getting illogical. The only threat to Miss Fraser, as far as we knew, came from the guy who had performed on the coffee, and surely we hadn't told him anything he didn't already know.

I had to usher Tully Strong to the door and out. If he had been capable of calming down enough to be seated for a talk I would have been all for it, but he was really upset. When Wolfe told me to put him out I couldn't conscientiously object. At that he had spunk. Anybody could have told from one glance at us that if I was forced to deal with him physically I would have had to decide what to do with my other hand, in case I wanted to be fully occupied, but when I took hold of his arm he jerked loose and then turned on me as if stretching me out would be pie. He had his specs in one hand, too. I succeeded in herding him out without either of us getting hurt.

As was to be expected, Tully Strong wasn't the only one who had the notion that Wolfe had committed treason by giving their fatal secret to the cops. They all let us know it, too, either by phone or in person. Nat Traub's attitude was specially bitter, probably because of the item that had been volunteered by Bill Meadows, that Traub had served the bottle and glass to Orchard. Cramer's crew must have really liked that one, and I could imagine the different keys they used playing it for Traub to hear. One thing I prefrered not to imagine was what we would have got from Mr. Walter B. Anderson, the Hi-Spot president, and Fred Owen, the director of public relations, if anyone had told them the full extent of Wolfe's treachery. Apparently they were still ignorant about the truth and horrible reason why one of the bottles had contained coffee instead of The Drink You Dream Of.

Another caller, this one Monday afternoon, was the formula hound, Professor Savarese. He too came to the office straight from a long conference with the cops, and he too was good and mad, but for a different reason. The cops had no longer been interested in his association with Cyril Orchard, or in anything about Orchard at all, and he wanted to know why. They had refused to tell him. They had reviewed his whole life, from birth to date, all over again, but with an entirely different approach. It was plain that what they were after now was a link between him and Miss Fraser. Why? What new factor had entered? The intrusion of a hitherto unknown and unsuspected factor would raise hell with his calculation of probabilities, but if there was one he had to have it, and quick. This was the first good chance he had ever had to test his formulas on the most dramatic of all problems, a murder case, from the inside, and he wasn't going to tolerate any blank spaces without a fight.

What was the new factor? Why was it now a vital question whether he had had any previous association, direct or indirect, with Miss Fraser?

Up to a point Wolfe listened to him without coming to a boil, but he finally got annoyed enough to call on me again to do some more ushering. I obeyed in a halfhearted way. For one thing, Wolfe was passing up another chance to do a dime's worth of work himself, with Savarese right there and more than ready to talk, and for another, I was resisting a temptation. The question had popped into my head, how would this figure wizard go about getting Miss Fraser's indigestion into a mathematical equation? It might not be instructive to get him to answer it, but at least it would pass the time, and it would help as much in solving the case as anything Wolfe was doing. But, not wanting to get us any more deeply involved in treachery than we already were, I skipped it.

I ushered him out.

Anyhow, that was only Monday. By the time four more days had passed and another Friday arrived, finishing a full week since we had supplied Cramer with a fact, I was a promising prospect for a strait jacket. That evening, as I returned to the office with Wolfe after an unusually good dinner which I had not enjoyed, the outlook for the next three or four hours revolted me. As he got himself adjusted comfortably in his chair and reached for his book, I announced:

"I'm going to my club."

He nodded, and got his book open.

"You do not even," I said cuttingly, "ask me which club, though you know damn well I don't belong to any. I am thoroughly fed up with sitting here day after day and night after night, waiting for the moment when the idea will somehow seep into you that a detective is supposed to detect. You are simply too goddam lazy to live. You think you're a genius. Say you are. If in order to be a genius myself I had to be as self-satisfied, as overweight, and as inert as you are, I like me better this way."

Apparently he was reading.

"This," I said, "is the climax I've been leading up to for a week—or rather, that you've been leading me up to. Sure, I know your alibi, and I'm good and sick of it—that there is nothing we can do that the cops aren't already doing. Of all the sausage." I kept my voice dry, factual, and cultured. "If this case is too much for you why don't you try another one? The papers are full of them. How about the gang that stole a truckload of cheese yesterday right here on Eleventh Avenue? How about the fifth-grade boy that hit his teacher in the eye with a jelly bean? Page fifty-eight in the *Times*. Or, if everything but murder is beneath you, what's wrong with the political and economic fortune-teller, a lady named Beula Poole, who got shot in the back of her head last evening? Page one of any paper. You could probably sew that one up before bedtime."

He turned over a page.

"Tomorrow," I said, "is Saturday. I shall draw my pay as usual. I'm going to a fight at the Garden. Talk about contrasts —you in that chair and a couple of good middleweights in a ring."

I blew.

But I didn't go to the Garden. My first stop was the corner drugstore, where I went to a phone booth and called Lon Cohen of the *Gazette*. He was in, and about through, and saw no reason why I shouldn't buy him eight or ten drinks, provided he could have a two-inch steak for a chaser.

So an hour later Lon and I were at a corner table at Pietro's. He had done well with the drinks and had made a good start on the steak. I was having highballs, to be sociable, and was on my third, along with my second pound of peanuts. I hadn't realized how much I had short-changed myself on dinner, sitting opposite Wolfe, until I got into the spirit of it with the peanuts.

We had discussed the state of things from politics to prize-fights, by no means excluding murder. Lon had had his glass filled often enough, and had enough of the steak in him, to have reached a state of mind where he might reasonably be expected to be open to suggestion. So I made an approach by telling him, deadpan, that in my opinion the papers were riding the cops too hard on the Orchard case.

He leered at me. "For God's sake, has Cramer threatened to take your license or something?"

"No, honest," I insisted, reaching for peanuts, "this one is really tough and you know it. They're doing as well as they can with what they've got. Besides that, it's so damn commonplace. Every paper always does it—after a week start crabbing and after two weeks start screaming. It's got so everybody always expects it and nobody ever reads it. You know what I'd do if I ran a newspaper? I'd start running stuff that people would read."

"Jesus!" Lon gawked at me. "What an idea! Give me a column on it. Who would teach 'em to read?"

"A column," I said, "would only get me started. I need at least a page. But in this particular case, where it's at now, it's a question of an editorial. This is Friday night. For Sunday you ought to have an editorial on the Orchard case. It's still hot and the public still loves it. But—"

"I'm no editor, I'm a news man."

"I know, I'm just talking. Five will get you ten that your sheet will have an editorial on the Orchard case Sunday, and what will it say? It will be called OUR PUBLIC GUARDIANS, and it will be the same old crap, and not one in a thousand will read beyond the first line. Phooey. If it was me I would call it TOO OLD OR TOO FAT, and I wouldn't mention the cops once. Nor would I mention Nero Wolfe, not by name. I would refer to the blaze of publicity with which a certain celebrated private investigator entered the Orchard case, and to the expectations it aroused. That his record seemed to justify it. That we see now how goofy it was, because in ten days he hasn't taken a trick. That the reason may be that he is getting too old, or too fat, or merely that he hasn't got what it takes when a case is really tough, but no matter what the reason is, this shows us that for our protection from vicious criminals we must rely on our efficient and well-trained police force, and not on any so-called brilliant geniuses. I said I wouldn't mention the cops, but I think I'd better, right at the last. I could add a sentence that while they may have got stuck in the mud on the Orchard case, they are the brave men who keep the structure of our society from you know."

Lon, having swallowed a hunk of steak, would have spoken, but I stopped him:

"They would read that, don't think they wouldn't. I know you're not an editor, but you're the best man they've got and you're allowed to talk to editors, aren't you? I would love to see an editorial like that tried, just as an experiment. So much so that if a paper ran it I would want to show my appreciation the first opportunity I get, by stretching a point a hell of a ways to give it first crack at some interesting little item."

Lon had his eyebrows up. "If you don't want to bore me, turn it the other side up so the interesting little item will be on top."

"Nuts. Do you want to talk about it or not?"

"Sure, I'll talk about anything."

I signaled the waiter for refills.

14

I WOULD give anything in the world, anyway up to four bits, to know whether Wolfe saw or read that editorial before I showed it to him late Sunday afternoon. I think he did. He always glances over the editorials in three papers, of which the *Gazette* is one, and if his eye caught it at all he must have read it. It was entitled THE FALSE ALARM, and it carried out the idea I had given Lon to a T.

I knew of course that Wolfe wouldn't do any spluttering, and I should have realized that he probably wouldn't make any sign or offer any comment. But I didn't, and therefore by late afternoon I was in a hole. If he hadn't read it I had to see that he did, and that was risky. It had to be done right or he would smell an elephant. So I thought it over: what would be the natural thing? How would I naturally do it if I suddenly ran across it?

What I did do was turn in my chair to grin at him and ask casually:

"Did you see this editorial in the *Gazette* called THE FALSE ALARM?"

He grunted. "What's it about?"

"You'd better read it." I got up, crossed over, and put it on his desk. "A funny thing, it gave me the feeling I had written it myself. It's the only editorial I've seen in weeks that I completely agree with."

He picked it up. I sat down facing him, but he held the paper so that it cut off my view. He isn't a fast reader, and he held the pose long enough to read it through twice, but that's exactly what he would have done if he already knew it by heart and wanted me to think otherwise.

"Bah!" The paper was lowered. "Some little scrivener who doubtless has ulcers and is on a diet."

"Yeah, I guess so. The rat. The contemptible louse. If only he knew how you've been sweating and stewing, going without sleep—"

"Archie. Shut up."

"Yes, sir."

I hoped to God I was being natural.

That was all for then, but I was not licked. I had never supposed that he would tear his hair or pace up and down. A little later an old friend of his, Marko Vukcić dropped in for a Sunday evening snack—five kinds of cheese, guava jelly, freshly roasted chestnuts, and almond tarts. I was anxious to see if he would show the editorial to Marko, which would have been a bad sign. He didn't. After Marko had left, to return to Rusterman's Restaurant, which was the best in New York because he managed it, Wolfe settled down with his book again, but hadn't turned more than ten pages before he dogeared and closed it and tossed it to a far corner of his desk. He then got up, crossed the room to the big globe, and stood and studied geography. That didn't seem to satisfy him any better than the book, so he went and turned on the radio. After dialing to eight different stations, he muttered to himself, stalked back to his chair behind his desk, and sat and scowled. I took all this in only from a corner of one eye, since I was buried so deep in a magazine that I didn't even know he was in the room.

He spoke. "Archie."

"Yes, sir?"

"It has been nine days."

"Yes, sir."

"Since that tour de force of yours. Getting that Miss Shepherd here."

"Yes, sir."

He was being tactful. What he meant was that it had been nine days since he had passed a miracle by uncovering the tape on the bottle and Miss Fraser's indigestion, but he figured that if he tossed me a bone I would be less likely either to snarl or to gloat. He went on:

"It was not then flighty to assume that a good routine job was all that was needed. But the events of those nine days have not supported that assumption."

"No, sir."

"Get Mr. Cramer."

"As soon as I finish this paragraph."

I allowed a reasonable number of seconds to go by, but I admit I wasn't seeing a word. Then, getting on the phone, I was prepared to settle for less than the inspector himself, since it was Sunday evening, and hoped that Wolfe was too, but it wasn't necessary. Cramer was there, and Wolfe got on and invited him to pay us a call.

"I'm busy." Cramer sounded harassed. "Why, have you got something?"

"Yes."

"What?"

"I don't know. I won't know until I've talked with you. After we've talked your busyness may be more productive than it has been."

"The hell you say. I'll be there in half an hour."

That didn't elate me at all. I hadn't cooked up a neat little scheme, and devoted a whole evening to it, and bought Lon Cohen twenty bucks' worth of liquids and solids, just to prod Wolfe into getting Cramer in to talk things over. As for his saying he had something, that was a plain lie. All he had was a muleheaded determination not to let his ease and comfort be interfered with.

So when Cramer arrived I didn't bubble over. Neither did he, for that matter. He marched into the office, nodded a greeting, dropped into the red leather chair, and growled:

"I wish to God you'd forget you're eccentric and start moving around more. Busy as I am, here I am. What is it?"

"My remark on the phone," Wolfe said placidly, "may have been blunt, but it was justified."

"What remark?"

"That your busyness could be more productive. Have you made any progress?"

"No."

"You're no further along than you were a week ago?"

86

"Further along to the day I retire, yes. Otherwise no."

"Then I'd like to ask some questions about that woman, Beula Poole, who was found dead in her office Friday morning. The papers say that you say it was murder. Was it?"

I gawked at him. This was clear away from me. When he jumped completely off the track like that I never knew whether he was stalling, being subtle, or trying to show me how much of a clod I was. Then I saw a gleam in Cramer's eye which indicated that even he had left me far behind, and all I could do was gawk some more.

Cramer nodded. "Yeah, it was murder. Why, looking for another client so I can earn another fee for you?"

"Do you know who did it?"

"No."

"No glimmer? No good start?"

"No start at all, good or bad."

"Tell me about it."

Cramer grunted. "Most of it has been in the papers, all but a detail or two we've saved up." He moved further back in the chair, as if he might stay longer than he had thought. "First you might tell me what got you interested, don't you think?"

"Certainly. Mr. Cyril Orchard, who got killed, was the publisher of a horse race tip sheet for which subscribers paid ten dollars a week, an unheard-of price. Miss Beula Poole, who also got killed was the publisher of a sheet which purported to give inside advance information on political and economic affairs, for which subscribers paid the same unheard-of price of ten dollars a week."

"Is that all?"

"I think it's enough to warrant a question or two. It is true that Mr. Orchard was poisoned and Miss Poole was shot, a big variation in method. Also that it is now assumed that Mr. Orchard was killed by misadventure, the poison having been intended for another, whereas the bullet that killed Miss Poole must have been intended for her. But even so, it's a remarkable coincidence—sufficiently so to justify some curiosity, at least. For example, it might be worth the trouble to compare the lists of subscribers of the two publications."

"Yeah, I thought so too."

"You did?" Wolfe was a little annoyed, as he always was at any implication that someone else could be as smart as him. "Then you've compared them. And?"

Cramer shook his head. "I didn't say I'd compared them, I

said I'd thought of it. What made me think of it was the fact that it couldn't be done, because there weren't any lists to compare."

"Nonsense. There must have been. Did you look for them?"

"Sure we did, but too late. In Orchard's case there was a little bad management. His office, a little one-room hole in a building on Forty-second Street, was locked, and there was some fiddling around looking for an employee or a relative to let us in. When we finally entered by having the superintendent admit us, the next day, the place had been cleaned out—not a piece of paper or an address plate or anything else. It was different with the woman, Poole, because it was in her office that she was shot—another one-room hole, on the third floor of an old building on Nineteenth Street, only four blocks from my place. But her body wasn't found until nearly noon the next day, and by the time we got there that had been cleaned out too. The same way. Nothing."

Wolfe was no longer annoyed. Cramer had had two coincidences and he had had only one. "Well." He was purring. "That settles it. In spite of variations, it is now more than curiosity. Of course you have inquired?"

"Plenty. The sheets were printed at different shops, and neither of them had a list of subscribers or anything else that helps. Neither Orchard nor the woman employed any help. Orchard left a widow and two children, but they don't seem to know a damn thing about his business, let alone who his subscribers were. Beula Poole's nearest relatives live out West, in Colorado, and they don't know anything, apparently not even how she was earning a living. And so on. As for the routine, all covered and all useless. No one seen entering or leaving—it's only two flights up—no weapon, no fingerprints that help any, nobody heard the shot—"

Wolfe nodded impatiently. "You said you hadn't made any start, and naturally routine has been followed. Any discoverable association of Miss Poole with Mr. Orchard?"

"If there was we can't discover it."

"Where were Miss Fraser and the others at the time Miss Poole was shot?"

Cramer squinted at him. "You think it might even develop that way?"

"I would like to put the question. Wouldn't you?"

"Yeah. I have. You see, the two offices being cleaned out is a detail we've saved up." Cramer looked at me. "And you'll kindly not peddle it to your pal Cohen of the *Gazette*." He went on to Wolfe: "It's not so easy because there's a leeway of four or five hours on when she was shot. We've asked all that bunch about it, and no one can be checked off."

"Mr. Savarese? Miss Shepherd? Mr. Shepherd?"

"What?" Cramer's eyes widened. "Where the hell does Shepherd come in?"

"I don't know. Archie doesn't like him, and I have learned that it is always quite possible that anyone he doesn't like may be a murderer."

"Oh, comic relief. The Shepherd girl was in Atlantic City with her mother, and still is. On Savarese I'd have to look at the reports, but I know he's not checked off because nobody is. By the way, we've dug up two subscribers to Orchard's tip sheet, besides Savarese and the Fraser woman. With no result. They bet on the races and they subscribed, that's all, according to them."

"I'd like to talk with them," Wolfe declared.

"You can. At my office any time."

"Pfui. As you know, I never leave this house on business. If you'll give Archie their names and addresses he'll attend to it."

Cramer said he'd have Stebbins phone and give them to me. I never saw him more cooperative, which meant that he had never been more frustrated.

They kept at it a while longer, but Cramer had nothing more of any importance to give Wolfe, and Wolfe hadn't had anything to give Cramer to begin with. I listened with part of my brain, and with the other part tried to do a little offhand sorting and arranging. I had to admit that it would take quite a formula to have room for the two coincidences as such, and therefore they would probably have to be joined together somehow, but it was no part-brain job for me. Whenever dough passes without visible value received the first thing you think of is blackmail, so I thought of it, but that didn't get me anywhere because there were too many other things in the way. It was obvious that the various aspects were not yet in a condition that called for the application of my particular kind of talent.

After Cramer had gone Wolfe sat and gazed at a distant corner of the ceiling with his eyes open about a thirty-second of an inch. I sat and waited, not wanting to disturb him, for when I saw his lips pushing out, and in again, and out and in, I knew he was exerting himself to the limit, and I was perfectly satisfied. There had been a good chance that he would figure that he had helped all he could for a while, and go back to his reading until Cramer made a progress report or somebody else got killed. But the editorial had stung him good. Finally he transferred the gaze to me and pronounced my name.

"Yes, sir," I said brightly.

"Your notebook. Take this."

I got ready.

"Former subscribers to the publication of Cyril Orchard, or to that of Beula Poole, should communicate with me immediately. Put it in three papers, the *Gazette*, the *News*, and the *Herald-Tribune*. A modest display, say two inches. Reply to a box number. A good page if possible."

"And I'll call for the replies? It saves time."

"Then do so."

I put paper in the typewriter. The phone rang. It was Sergeant Purley Stebbins, to give me the names and addresses of the two Orchard subscribers they had dug up.

15

So BEGINNING Monday morning we were again a going concern, instead of a sitting-and-waiting one, but I was not in my element. I like a case you can make a diagram of. I don't object to complications, that's all right, but if you're out for bear it seems silly to concentrate on hunting for moose tracks. Our fee depended on our finding out how and why Orchard got cyanided by drinking Madeline Fraser's sugared coffee, and here we were spending our time and energy on the shooting of a female named Beula Poole. Even granting it was one and the same guy who pinched the lead pencils and spilled ink on the rug, if you've been hired to nail him for pencil stealing that's what you should work at.

I admit that isn't exactly fair, because most of our Monday activities had to do with Orchard. Wolfe seemed to think it was important for him to have a talk with those two subscribers, so instead of using the phone I went out after them. I had one of them in the office waiting for him at 11:00 A.M.—an assistant office manager for a big tile company. Wolfe spent less than a quarter of an hour on him, knowing, of course, that the cops had spent more and had checked him. He had bet on the races for years. In February a year ago he had learned that a Hialeah daily double featured in a sheet called *Track Almanac* had come through for a killing, and he had subscribed, though the ten bucks a week was a sixth of his salary. He had stayed with it for nine weeks and then quit. So much for him.

The other one was a little different. Her name was Marie Leconne, and she owned a snooty beauty parlor on Madison Avenue. She wouldn't have accepted my invitation if she hadn't been under the illusion that Wolfe was connected with the police, though I didn't precisely tell her so. That Monday evening she was with us a good two hours, but left nothing of any value behind. She had subscribed to *Track Almanac* in August, seven months ago, and had remained a subscriber up to the time of Orchard's death. Prior to subscribing she had done little or no betting on the races; she was hazy about whether it was little, or no. Since subscribing she had bet frequently, but she firmly refused to tell where, through whom, or in what amounts. Wolfe, knowing that I occasionally risk a finif, passed me a hint to have some conversation with her about pertinent matters like horses and jockeys, but she declined to cooperate. All in all, she kept herself nicely under control, and flew off the handle only once, when Wolfe pressed her hard for a plausible reason why she had subscribed to a tip sheet at such a price. That aggravated her terribly, and since the one thing that scares Wolfe out of his senses is a woman in a tantrum, he backed away fast.

He did keep on trying, from other angles, but when she finally left all we knew for sure was that she had not subscribed to *Track Almanac* in order to get guesses on the ponies. She was slippery, and nobody's fool, and Wolfe had got no further than the cops in opening her up.

I suggested to Wolfe: "We might start Saul asking around in her circle."

He snorted. "Mr. Cramer is presumably attending to that, and, anyway, it would have to be dragged out of her inch by inch. The advertisement should be quicker."

It was quicker, all right, in getting results, but not the results we were after. There had not been time to make the Monday papers, so the ad's first appearance was Tuesday morning. Appraising it, I thought it caught the eye effectively for so small a space. After breakfast, which I always eat in the kitchen with Fritz while Wolfe has his in his room on a tray, and after dealing with the morning mail and other chores in the office, I went out to stretch my legs and thought I might as well head in the direction of the Herald-

Tribune Building. Expecting nothing so soon but thinking it wouldn't hurt to drop in, I did so. There was a telegram. I tore it open and read:

CALL MIDLAND FIVE THREE SEVEN
EIGHT FOUR LEAVE MESSAGE FOR
DUNCAN GIVING APPOINTMENT

I went to a phone booth and put a nickel in the slot, with the idea of calling Cramer's office to ask who Midland 5-3784 belonged to, but changed my mind. If it happened that this led to a hot trail we didn't want to be hampered by city interference, at least I didn't. However, I thought I might as well get something for my nickel and dialed another number. Fritz answered, and I asked him to switch it to the plant rooms.

"Yes, Archie?" Wolfe's voice came, peevish. He was at the bench repotting, as I knew from his schedule, and he hates to be interrupted at that job. I told him about the telegram.

"Very well, call the number. Make an appointment for eleven o'clock or later."

I walked back home, went to my desk, dialed the Midland number, and asked for Mr. Duncan. Of course it could have been Mrs. or Miss, but I preferred to deal with a man after our experience with Marie Leconne. A gruff voice with an accent said that Mr. Duncan wasn't there and was there a message.

"Will he be back soon?"

"I don't know. All I know is that I can take a message."

I thereupon delivered one, that Mr. Duncan would be expected at Nero Wolfe's office at eleven o'clock, or as soon thereafter as possible.

He didn't come. Wolfe descended in his elevator sharp at eleven as usual, got himself enthroned, rang for beer, and began sorting plant cards he had brought down with him. I had him sign a couple of checks and then started to help with the cards. At half past eleven I asked if I should ring the Midland number to see if Duncan had got the message, and he said no, we would wait until noon.

The phone rang. I went to my desk and told it:

"Nero Wolfe's office, Goodwin speaking."

"I got your message for Duncan. Let me speak to Mr. Wolfe, please."

I covered the transmitter and told Wolfe: "He says Duncan, but it's a voice I've heard. It's not a familiar voice, but by God I've heard it. See if you have."

Wolfe lifted his instrument.

"Yes, Mr. Duncan? This is Nero Wolfe."

"How are you?" the voice asked.

"I'm well, thank you. Do I know you, sir?"

"I really don't know. I mean I don't know if you would recognize me, seeing me, because I don't know how foolishly inquisitive you may have been. But we have talked before, on the phone."

"We have?"

"Yes. Twice. On June ninth, nineteen forty-three, I called to give you some advice regarding a job you were doing for General Carpenter. On January sixteenth, nineteen forty-six, I called to speak about the advisability of limiting your efforts in behalf of a Mrs. Tremont."

"Yes. I remember."

I remembered too. I chalked it against me that I hadn't recognized the voice with the first six words, though it had been over two years since I had heard it—hard, slow, precise, and cold as last week's corpse. It was continuing:

"I was pleased to see that you did limit your efforts as I suggested. That showed—"

"I limited them because no extension of them was required to finish the job I was hired for. I did not limit them because you suggested it, Mr. Zeck." Wolfe was being fairly icy himself.

"So you know my name." The voice never changed.

"Certainly. I went to some trouble and expense to ascertain it. I don't pay much attention to threats, I get too many of them, but at least I like to know who the threatener is. Yes, I know your name, sir. Is that temerarious? Many people know Mr. Arnold Zeck."

"You have had no occasion to. This, Mr. Wolfe, does *not* please me."

"I didn't expect it to."

"No. But I am much easier to get along with when I am pleased. That's why I sent you that telegram and am talking with you now. I have strong admiration for you, as I've said before. I wouldn't want to lose it. It would please me better to keep it. Your advertisement in the papers has given me some concern. I realize that you didn't know that, you couldn't have known it, so I'm telling you. The advertisement disturbs me. It can't be recalled; it has appeared. But it is extremely important that you should not permit it to lead you into difficulties that will be too much for you. The wisest course for you will be to drop the matter. You understand me, don't you, Mr. Wolfe?"

"Oh yes, I understand you. You put things quite clearly, Mr. Zeck, and so do I. I have engaged to do something, and I intend to do it. I haven't the slightest desire either to please you or to displease you, and unless one or the other is inherent in my job you have no reason to be concerned. You understand me, don't you?"

"Yes. I do. But now you know."

The line went dead.

Wolfe cradled the phone and leaned back in his chair, with his eyes closed to a slit. I pushed my phone away, swiveled, and gazed at him through a minute's silence.

"So," I said. "That sonofabitch. Shall I find out about the Midland number?"

Wolfe shook his head. "Useless. It would be some little store that merely took a message. Anyway, he has a number of his own."

"Yeah. He didn't know you knew his name. Neither did I. How did that happen?"

"Two years ago I engaged some of Mr. Bascom's men without telling you. He had sounded as if he were a man of resource and resolution, and I didn't want to get you involved."

"It's the Zeck with the place in Westchester, of course?"

"Yes. I should have signaled you off as soon as I recognized his voice. I tell you nothing because it is better for you to know nothing. You are to forget that you know his name."

"Like that." I snapped my fingers, and grinned at him. "What the hell? Does he eat human flesh, preferably handsome young men?"

"No. He does worse." Wolfe's eyes came half open. "I'll tell you this. If ever, in the course of my business, I find that I am committed against him and must destroy him, I shall leave this house, find a place where I can work—and sleep and eat if there is time for it—and stay there until I have finished. I don't want to do that, and therefore I hope I'll never have to."

"I see. I'd like to meet this bozo. I think I'll make his acquaintance."

"You will not. You'll stay away from him." He made a

94

face. "If this job leads me to that extremity—well, it will or it won't." He glanced at the clock. "It's nearly noon. You'd better go and see if any more answers have arrived. Can't you telephone?"

16

THERE were no more answers. That goes not only for Tuesday noon, but for the rest of the day and evening, and Wednesday morning, and Wednesday after lunch. Nothing doing.

It didn't surprise me. The nature of the phone call from the man whose name I had been ordered to forget made it seem likely that there was something peculiar about the subscribers to *Track Almanac* and *What to Expect,* which was the name of the political and economic dope sheet published by the late Beula Poole. But even granting that there wasn't, that as far as they were concerned it was all clean and straight, the two publishers had just been murdered, and who would be goop enough to answer such an ad just to get asked a lot of impertinent questions? In the office after lunch Wednesday I made a remark to that effect to Wolfe, and got only a growl for reply.

"We might at least," I insisted, "have hinted that they would get their money back or something."

No reply.

"We could insert it again and add that. Or we could offer a reward for anyone who would give us the name of an Orchard or Poole subscriber."

No reply.

"Or I could go up to the Fraser apartment and get into conversation with the bunch, and who knows?"

"Yes. Do so."

I looked at him suspiciously. He meant it.

"Now?"

"Yes."

"You sure are hard up when you start taking suggestions from me."

I pulled the phone to me and dialed the number. It was Bill Meadows who answered, and he sounded anything but gay, even when he learned it was me. After a brief talk, however, I was willing to forgive him. I hung up and informed Wolfe:

"I guess I'll have to postpone it. Miss Fraser and Miss Koppel are both out. Bill was a little vague, but I gather that the latter has been tagged by the city authorities for some reason or other, and the former is engaged in trying to remove the tag. Maybe she needs help. Why don't I find out?"

"I don't know. You might try."

I turned and dialed Watkins 9-8241. Inspector Cramer wasn't available, but I got someone just as good, or sometimes I think even better, Sergeant Stebbins.

"I need some information," I told him, "in connection with this fee you folks are earning for Mr. Wolfe."

"So do we," he said frankly. "Got any?"

"Not right now. Mr. Wolfe and I are in conference. How did Miss Koppel hurt your feelings, and where is she, and if you see Miss Fraser give her my love."

He let out a roar of delight. Purley doesn't laugh often, at least when he's on duty, and I resented it. I waited until I thought he might hear me and then demanded:

"What the hell is so funny?"

"I never expected the day to come," he declared. "You calling me to ask where your client is. What's the matter, is Wolfe off his feed?"

"I know another one even better. Call me back when you're through laughing."

"I'm through. Haven't you heard what the Koppel dame did?"

"No. I only know what you tell me."

"Well, this isn't loose yet. We may want to keep it a while if we can, I don't know."

"I'll help you keep it. So will Mr. Wolfe."

"That's understood?"

"Yes."

"Okay. Of course they've all been told not to leave the jurisdiction. This morning Miss Koppel took a cab to LaGuardia. She was nabbed as she was boarding the nine o'clock plane for Detroit. She says she wanted to visit her sick mother in Fleetville, which is eighty miles from Detroit. But she didn't ask permission to go, and the word we get is that her mother is no sicker than she has been for a year. So we charged her as a material witness. Does that strike you as highhanded? Do you think it calls for a shakeup?"

"Get set for another laugh. Where's Miss Fraser?"

"With her lawyer at the D.A.'s office discussing bail."

"What kind of reasons have you got for Miss Koppel taking a trip that are any better than hers?"

"I wouldn't know. Now you're out of my class. If you want to go into details like that, Wolfe had better ask the Inspector."

I tried another approach or two, but either Purley had given me all there was or the rest was in another drawer which he didn't feel like opening. I hung up and relayed the news to Wolfe.

He nodded as if it were no concern of his. I glared at him:

"It wouldn't interest you to have one or both of them stop in for a chat on their way home? To ask why Miss Koppel simply had to go to Michigan would be vulgar curiosity?"

"Bah. The police are asking, aren't they?" Wolfe was bitter. "I've spent countless hours with those people, and got something for it only when I had a whip to snap. Why compound futility? I need another whip. Call those newspapers again."

"Am I still to go up there? After the ladies get home?"

"You might as well."

"Yeah." I was savage. "At least I can compound some futility."

I phoned all three papers. Nothing. Being in no mood to sit and concentrate on germination records, I announced that I was going out for a walk, and Wolfe nodded absently. When I got back it was after four o'clock and he had gone up to the plant rooms. I fiddled around, finally decided that I might as well concentrate on something and the germination records were all I had, and got Theodore's reports from the drawer, but then I thought why not throw away three more nickels? So I started dialing again.

Herald-Tribune, nothing. *News*, nothing. But the *Gazette* girl said yes, they had one. The way I went for my hat and headed for Tenth Avenue to grab a taxi, you might have thought I was on my way to a murder.

The driver was a philosopher. "You don't see many eager happy faces like yours nowadays," he told me.

"I'm on my way to my wedding."

He opened his mouth to speak again, then clamped it shut. He shook his head resolutely. "No. Why should I spoil it?"

I paid him off outside the *Gazette* building and went in and got my prize. It was a square pale-blue envelope, and the printed return on the flap said:

Inside was a single sheet matching the envelope, with small neat handwriting on it:

Box P304:
Regarding your advertisement, I am not a former subscriber to either of the publications, but I may be able to tell you something. You may write me, or call Lincoln 3-4808, but do not phone before ten in the morning or after five-thirty in the afternoon. That is important.

Hilda Michaels

It was still forty minutes this side of her deadline, so I went straight to a booth and dialed the number. A female voice answered. I asked to speak to Mrs. Michaels.

"This is Mrs. Michaels."

"This is the *Gazette* advertiser you wrote to, Box P304. I've just read—"

"What's your name?" She had a tendency to snap.

"My name is Goodwin, Archie Goodwin. I can be up there in fifteen minutes or less—"

"No, you can't. Anyway, you'd better not. Are you connected with the Police Department?"

"No. I work for Nero Wolfe. You may have heard of Nero Wolfe, the detective?"

"Of course. This isn't a convent. Was that his advertisement?"

"Yes. He—"

"Then why didn't he phone me?"

"Because I just got your note. I'm phoning from a booth in the *Gazette* building. You said not—"

"Well, Mr. Goodman, I doubt if I can tell Mr. Wolfe anything he would be interested in. I really doubt it."

"Maybe not," I conceded. "But he would be the best judge of that. If you don't want me to come up there, how would it be if you called on Mr. Wolfe at his office? West Thirty-fifth Street—it's in the phone book. Or I could run up now in a taxi and—"

"Oh, not now. Not today. I might be able to make it tomorrow—or Friday—"

I was annoyed. For one thing, I would just as soon be permitted to finish a sentence once in a while, and for another, apparently she had read the piece about Wolfe being hired to work on the Orchard case, and my name had been in it, and it had been spelled correctly. So I took on weight:

"You don't seem to realize what you've done, Mrs. Michaels. You—"

"Why, what have I done?"

"You have landed smack in the middle of a murder case. Mr. Wolfe and the police are more or less collaborating on it. He would like to see you about the matter mentioned in his advertisement, not tomorrow or next week, but quick. I think you ought to see him. If you try to put it off because you've begun to regret sending this note he'll be compelled to consult the police, and then what? Then you'll—"

"I didn't say I regret sending the note."

"No, but the way you—"

"I'll be at Mr. Wolfe's office by six o'clock."

"Good! Shall I come—"

I might have known better than to give her another chance to chop me off. She said that she was quite capable of getting herself transported, and I could well believe it.

17

THERE was nothing snappy about her appearance. The mink coat, and the dark red woolen dress made visible when the coat had been spread over the back of the red leather chair, unquestionably meant well, but she was not built to cooperate with clothes. There was too much of her and the distribution was all wrong. Her face was so well padded that there was no telling whether there were any bones underneath, and the creases were considerably more than skin deep. I didn't like her. From Wolfe's expression it was plain, to me, that he didn't like her. As for her, it was a safe bet that she didn't like anybody.

Wolfe rustled the sheet of pale-blue paper, glanced at it again, and looked at her. "You say here, madam, that you may be able to tell me something. Your caution is understandable and even commendable. You wanted to find out who had placed the advertisement before committing yourself. Now you know. There is no need—"

"That man threatened me," she snapped. "That's not the way to get me to tell something—if I have something to tell."

"I agree. Mr. Goodwin is headstrong. —Archie, withdraw the threat."

I did my best to grin at her as man to woman. "I take it back, Mrs. Michaels. I was so anxious—"

"If I tell you anything," she said to Wolfe, ignoring me, "it will be because I want to, and it will be completely confidential. Whatever you do about it, of course I have nothing to say about that, but you will give me your solemn word of honor that my name will not be mentioned to anyone. No one is to know I wrote you or came to see you or had anything to do with it."

Wolfe shook his head. "Impossible. Manifestly impossible. You are not a fool, madam, and I won't try to treat you as if you were. It is even conceivable that you might have to take the witness stand in a murder trial. I know nothing about it, because I don't know what you have to tell. Then how could I—"

"All right," she said, surrendering. "I see I made a mistake. I must be home by seven o'clock. Here's what I have to tell you: somebody I know was a subscriber to that *What to Expect* that was published by that woman, Beula Poole. I distinctly remember, one day two or three months ago, I saw a little stack of them somewhere—in some house or apartment or office. I've been trying to remember where it was, and I simply can't. I wrote you because I thought you might tell me something that would make me remember, and I'm quite willing to try, but I doubt if it will do any good."

"Indeed." Wolfe's expression was fully as sour as hers. "I said you're not a fool. I suppose you're prepared to stick to that under any circum—"

"Yes, I am."

"Even if Mr. Goodwin gets headstrong again and renews his threat?"

"That!" She was contemptuous.

"It's very thin, Mrs. Michaels. Even ridiculous. That you would go to the bother of answering that advertisement, and coming down here—"

"I don't mind being ridiculous."

"Then I have no alternative." Wolfe's lips tightened. He released them. "I accept your conditions. I agree, for myself and for Mr. Goodwin, who is my agent, that we will not disclose the source of our information, and that we will do our utmost to keep anyone from learning it. Should anyone ascertain it, it will be against our will and in spite of our precautions in good faith. We cannot guarantee; we can only promise; and we do so."

Her eyes had narrowed. "On your solemn word of honor."

"Good heavens. That ragged old patch? Very well. My solemn word of honor. Archie?"

"My solemn word of honor," I said gravely.

Her head made an odd ducking movement, reminding me of a fat-cheeked owl I had seen at the zoo getting ready to swoop on a mouse.

"My husband," she said, "has been a subscriber to that publication, *What to Expect,* for eight months."

But the owl had swooped because it was hungry, whereas she was swooping just to hurt. It was in her voice, which was still hers but quite different when she said the word husband.

"And that's ridiculous," she went on, "if you want something ridiculous. He hasn't the slightest interest in politics or industry or the stock market or anything like that. He is a successful doctor and all he ever thinks about is his work and his patients, especially his women patients. What would he want with a thing like that *What to Expect*? Why should he pay that Beula Poole money every week, month after month? I have my own money, and for the first few years after we married we lived on my income, but then he began to be successful, and now he doesn't need my money any more. And he doesn't—"

Abruptly she stood up. Apparently the habit had got so strong that sometimes she even interrupted herself. She was turning to pick up her coat.

"If you please," Wolfe said brusquely. "You have my word of honor and I want some details. What has your husband—"

"That's all," she snapped. "I don't intend to answer any silly questions. If I did you'd be sure to give me away, you wouldn't be smart enough not to, and the details don't matter. I've told you the one thing you need to know, and I only hope—"

She was proceeding with the coat, and I had gone to her to help.

"Yes, madam, what do you hope?"

She looked straight at him. "I hope you've got some brains. You don't look it."

She turned and made for the hall, and I followed. Over the years I have opened that front door to let many people out of that house, among them thieves, swindlers, murderers, and assorted crooks, but it has never been a greater pleasure than on that occasion. Added to everything else, I had noticed when helping her with her coat that her neck needed washing.

It had not been news to us that her husband was a successful doctor. Between my return to the office and her arrival there had been time for a look at the phone book, which had him as an M.D. with an office address in the Sixties just off Park Avenue, and for a call to Doc Vollmer. Vollmer had never met him, but knew his standing and reputation, which were up around the top. He had a good high-bracket practice, with the emphasis on gynecology.

Back in the office I remarked to Wolfe, "There goes my pendulum again. Lately I've been swinging toward the notion of getting myself a little woman, but good Godalmighty. Brother!"

He nodded, and shivered a little. "Yes. However, we can't reject it merely because it's soiled. Unquestionably her fact is a fact; otherwise she would have contrived an elaborate support for it." He glanced at the clock. "She said she had to be home by seven, so he may still be in his office. Try it."

I found the number and dialed it. The woman who answered firmly intended to protect her employer from harassment by a stranger, but I finally sold her.

Wolfe took it. "Dr. Michaels? This is Nero Wolfe, a detective. Yes, sir, so far as I know there is only one of that name. I'm in a little difficulty and would appreciate some help from you."

"I'm just leaving for the day, Mr. Wolfe. I'm afraid I couldn't undertake to give you medical advice on the phone." His voice was low, pleasant, and tired.

"It isn't medical advice I need, doctor. I want to have a talk with you about a publication called *What to Expect*, to which you subscribed. The difficulty is that I find it impractical to leave my house. I could send my assistant or a policeman to see you, or both, but I would prefer to discuss it with you myself, confidentially. I wonder if you could call on me this evening after dinner?"

Evidently the interrupting mania in the Michaels family was confined to the wife. Not only did he not interrupt, he didn't even take a cue. Wolfe tried again:

"Would that be convenient, sir?"

"If I could have another moment, Mr. Wolfe. I've had a hard day and am trying to think."

"By all means."

He took ten seconds. His voice came, even tireder:

"I suppose it would be useless to tell you to go to hell. I would prefer not to discuss it on the phone. I'll be at your office around nine o'clock."

"Good. Have you a dinner engagement, doctor?"

"An engagement? No. I'm dining at home. Why?"

"It just occurred to me—could I prevail on you to dine with me? You said you were just leaving for the day. I have a good cook. We are having fresh pork tenderloin, with all fiber removed, done in a casserole, with a sharp brown sauce moderately spiced. There will not be time to chambrer a claret properly, but we can have the chill off. We shall of course not approach our little matter until afterward, with the coffee—or even after that. Do you happen to know the brandy labeled Remisier? It is not common. I hope this won't shock you, but the way to do it is to sip it with bites of Fritz's apple pie. Fritz is my cook."

"I'll be damned. I'll be there—what's the address?"

Wolfe gave it to him, and hung up.

"I'll be damned too," I declared. "A perfect stranger? He may put horse-radish on oysters."

Wolfe grunted. "If he had gone home to eat with that creature things might have been said. Even to the point of repudiation by her and defiance by him. I thought it prudent to avoid that risk."

"Nuts. There's no such risk and you know it. What you're trying to avoid is to give anyone an excuse to think you're human. You were being kind to your fellow man and you'd rather be caught dead. The idea of the poor devil going home to dine with that female hyena was simply too much for your great big warm heart, and you were so damn impetuous you even committed yourself to letting him have some of that brandy of which there are only nineteen bottles in the United States and they're all in your cellar."

"Bosh." He arose. "You would sentimentalize the multiplication table." He started for the kitchen, to tell Fritz about the guest, and to smell around.

18

AFTER dinner Fritz brought us a second pot of coffee in the office, and also the brandy bottle and big-bellied glasses. Most of the two hours had been spent, not on West Thirty-fifth Street in New York, but in Egypt. Wolfe and the guest had both spent some time there in days gone by, and they had settled on that for discussion and a few arguments.

Dr. Michaels, informally comfortable in the red leather chair, put down his coffee cup, ditched a cigarette, and gently patted his midriff. He looked exactly like a successful Park Avenue doctor, middle-aged, well-built and well-dressed, worried but self-assured. After the first hour at the table the tired and worried look had gone, but now, as he cocked an eye at Wolfe after disposing of the cigarette, his forehead was wrinkled again.

"This has been a delightful recess," he declared. "It has done me a world of good. I have dozens of patients for whom I would like to prescribe a dinner with you, but I'm afraid I'd have to advise you not to fill the prescription." He belched, and was well-mannered enough not to try to cheat on it. "Well. Now I'll stop masquerading as a guest and take my proper role. The human sacrifice."

Wolfe disallowed it. "I have no desire or intention to gut you, sir."

Michaels smiled. "A surgeon might say that too, as he slits the skin. No, let's get it done. Did my wife phone you, or write you, or come to see you?"

"You wife?" Wolfe's eyes opened innocently. "Has there been any mention of your wife?"

"Only by me, this moment. Let it pass. I suppose your solemn word of honor has been invoked—a fine old phrase, really, solemn word of honor—" He shrugged. "I wasn't actually surprised when you asked me about that blackmail business on the phone, merely momentarily confused. I had been expecting something of the sort, because it didn't seem likely that such an opportunity to cause me embarrassment —or perhaps worse—would be missed. Only I would have guessed it would be the police. This is much better, much."

Wolfe's head dipped forward, visibly, to acknowledge the

compliment. "It may eventually reach the police, doctor. There may be no help for it."

"Of course, I realize that. I can only hope not. Did she give you the anonymous letters, or just show them to you?"

"Neither. But that 'she' is your pronoun, not mine. With that understood—I have no documentary evidence, and have seen none. If there is some, no doubt I could get it." Wolfe sighed, leaned back, and half closed his eyes. "Wouldn't it be simpler if you assume that I know nothing at all, and tell me about it?"

"I suppose so, damn it." Michaels sipped some brandy, used his tongue to give all the membranes a chance at it, swallowed, and put the glass down. "From the beginning?"

"If you please."

"Well . . . it was last summer, nine months ago, that I first learned about the anonymous letters. One of my colleagues showed me one that he had received by mail. It strongly hinted that I was chronically guilty of—uh, unethical conduct—with women patients. Not long after that I became aware of a decided change in the attitude of one of my oldest and most valued patients. I appealed to her to tell me frankly what had caused it. She had received two similar letters. It was the next day—naturally my memory is quite vivid on this—that my wife showed me two letters, again similar, that had come to her."

The wrinkles on his forehead had taken command again. "I don't have to explain what that sort of thing could do to a doctor if it kept up. Of course I thought of the police, but the risk of possible publicity, or even spreading of rumor, through a police inquiry, was too great. There was the same objection, or at least I thought there was, to hiring a private investigator. Then, the day after my wife showed me the letters—no, two days after—I had a phone call at my home in the evening. I presume my wife listened to it on the extension in her room—but you're not interested in that. I wish to God you were—" Michaels abruptly jerked his head up as if he had heard a noise somewhere. "Now what did I mean by that?"

"I have no idea," Wolfe murmured. "The phone call?"

"It was a woman's voice. She didn't waste any words. She said she understood that people had been getting letters about me, and if it annoyed me and I wanted to stop it I could easily do so. If I would subscribe for one year to a publication called *What to Expect*—she gave me the address—there would be no more letters. The cost would be ten dollars a week, and I could pay as I pleased, weekly, monthly, or the year in advance. She assured me emphatically that there would be no request for renewal, that nothing beyond the one year's subscription would be required, that the letters would stop as soon as I subscribed, and that there would be no more."

Michaels turned a hand to show a palm. "That's all. I subscribed. I sent ten dollars a week for a while—eight weeks—and then I sent a check for four hundred and forty dollars. So far as I know there have been no more letters—and I think I would know."

"Interesting," Wolfe murmured. "Extremely."

"Yes," Michaels agreed. "I can understand your saying that. It's what a doctor says when he runs across something rare like a lung grown to a rib. But if he's tactful he doesn't say it in the hearing of the patient."

"You're quite right, sir. I apologize. But this is indeed a rarity—truly remarkable! If the execution graded as high as the conception . . . what were the letters like, typed?"

"Yes. Plain envelopes and plain cheap paper, but the typing was perfect."

"You said you sent a check. That was acceptable?"

Michaels nodded. "She made that clear. Either check or money order. Cash would be accepted, but was thought inadvisable on account of the risk in the mails."

"You see? Admirable. What about her voice?"

"It was medium in pitch, clear and precise, educated—I mean good diction and grammar—and matter-of-fact. One day I called the number of the publication—as you probably know, it's listed—and asked for Miss Poole. It was Miss Poole talking, she said. I discussed a paragraph in the latest issue, and she was intelligent and informed about it. But her voice was soprano, jerky and nervous, nothing like the voice that had told me how to get the letters stopped."

"It wouldn't be. That was what you phoned for?"

"Yes. I thought I'd have that much satisfaction at least, since there was no risk in it."

"You might have saved your nickel." Wolfe grimaced. "Dr. Michaels, I'm going to ask you a question."

"Go ahead."

"I don't want to, but though the question is intrusive it is also important. And it will do no good to ask it unless I can be assured of a completely candid reply or a refusal to answer at all. You would be capable of a fairly good job of evasion if you were moved to try, and I don't want that. Will you give me either candor or silence?"

Michaels smiled. "Silence is so awkward. I'll give you a straight answer or I'll say 'no comment.'"

"Good. How much substance was there in the hints in those letters about your conduct?"

The doctor looked at him, considered, and finally nodded his head. "It's intrusive, all right, but I'll take your word for it that it's important. You want a full answer?"

"As full as possible."

"Then it must be confidential."

"It will be."

"I accept that. I don't ask for your solemn word of honor. There was not even a shadow of substance. I have never, with any patient, even approached the boundaries of professional decorum. But I'm not like you; I have a deep and intense need for the companionship of a woman. I suppose that's why I married so early—and so disastrously. Possibly her money attracted me too, though I would vigorously deny it; there are bad streaks in me. Anyway, I do have the companionship of a woman, but not the one I married. She has never been my patient. When she needs medical advice she goes to some other doctor. No doctor should assume responsibility for the health of one he loves or one he hates."

"This companionship you enjoy—it could not have been the stimulus for the hints in the letters?"

"I don't see how. All the letters spoke of women patients —in the plural, and patients."

"Giving their names?"

"No, no names."

Wolfe nodded with satisfaction. "That would have taken too much research for a wholesale operation, and it wasn't necessary." He came forward in his chair to reach for the push button. "I am greatly obliged to you, Dr. Michaels. This has been highly distasteful for you, and you have been most indulgent. I don't need to prolong it, and I won't. I foresee no necessity to give the police your name, and I'll even engage not to do so, though heaven only knows what my informant will do. Now we'll have some beer. We didn't get it settled about the pointed arches in the Tulun mosque."

"If you don't mind," the guest said, "I've been wondering if it would be seemly to tip this brandy bottle again."

So he stayed with the brandy while Wolfe had beer. I excused myself and went out for a breath of air, for while they were perfectly welcome to do some more settling about the pointed arches in the Tulun mosque, as far as I was concerned it had been attended to long ago.

It was past eleven when I returned, and soon afterward Michaels arose to go. He was far from being pickled, but he was much more relaxed and rosy than he had been when I let him in. Wolfe was so mellow that he even stood up to say good-by, and I didn't see his usual flicker of hesitation when Michaels extended a hand. He doesn't care about shaking hands indiscriminately.

Michaels said impulsively, "I want to ask you something."

"Then do so."

"I want to consult you professionally—your profession. I need help. I want to pay for it."

"You will, sir, if it's worth anything."

"It will be, I'm sure. I want to know, if you are being shadowed, if a man is following you, how many ways are there of eluding him, and what are they, and how are they executed?"

"Good heavens." Wolfe shuddered. "How long has this been going on?"

"For months."

"Well. —Archie?"

"Sure," I said. "Glad to."

"I don't want to impose on you," Michaels lied. He did. "It's late."

"That's okay. Sit down."

I really didn't mind, having met his wife.

19

THAT, I thought to myself as I was brushing my hair Thursday morning, covered some ground. That was a real step forward.

Then, as I dropped the brush into the drawer, I asked aloud, "Yeah? Toward what?"

In a murder case you expect to spend at least half your time barking up wrong trees. Sometimes that gets you irritated, but what the hell, if you belong in the detective business at all you just skip it and take another look. That wasn't the trouble with this one. We hadn't gone dashing around investigating a funny sound only to learn it was just a cat on a fence. Far from it. We had left all that to the cops. Every move we had made had been strictly pertinent. Our two chief discoveries—the tape on the bottle of coffee and the way the circulation department of *What to Expect* operated—were unquestionably essential parts of the picture of the death of Cyril Orchard, which was what we were working on.

So it was a step forward. Fine. When you have taken a step forward, the next thing on the program is another step in the same direction. And that was the pebble in the griddle cake I broke a tooth on that morning. Bathing and dressing and eating breakfast, I went over the situation from every angle and viewpoint, and I had to admit this: if Wolfe had called me up to his room and asked for a suggestion on how I should spend the day, I would have been tongue-tied.

What I'm doing, if you're following me, is to justify what I did do. When he did call me up to his room, and wished me a good morning, and asked how I had slept, and told me to phone Inspector Cramer and invited him to pay us a visit at eleven o'clock, all I said was:

"Yes, sir."

There was another phone call which I had decided to make on my own. Since it involved a violation of a law Wolfe had passed I didn't want to make it from the office, so when I went out for a stroll to the bank to deposit a check from a former client who was paying in installments, I patronized a booth. When I got Lon Cohen I told him I wanted to ask him something that had no connection with the detective business, but was strictly private. I said I had been offered a job at a figure ten times what he was worth, and fully half what I was, and, while I had no intention of leaving Wolfe, I was curious. Had he ever heard of a guy named Arnold Zeck, and what about him?

"Nothing for you," Lon said.

"What do you mean, nothing for me?"

"I mean you don't want a Sunday feature, you want the lowdown, and I haven't got it. Zeck is a question mark. I've heard that he owns twenty Assemblymen and six district leaders, and I've also heard that he is merely a dried fish. There's a rumor that if you print something about him that he resents your body is washed ashore at Montauk Point, mangled by sharks, but you know how the boys talk. One little detail—this is between us?"

"Forever."

"There's not a word on him in our morgue. I had occasion to look once, several years ago—when he gave his yacht to the Navy. Not a thing, which is peculiar for a guy that gives away yachts and owns the highest hill in Westchester. What's the job?"

"Skip it. I wouldn't consider it. I thought he still had his yacht."

I decided to let it lay. If the time should come when Wolfe had to sneak outdoors and look for a place to hide, I didn't want it blamed on me.

Cramer arrived shortly after eleven. He wasn't jovial, and neither was I. When he came, as I had known him to, to tear Wolfe to pieces, or at least to threaten to haul him downtown or send a squad with a paper signed by a judge, he had fire in his eye and springs in his calves. This time he was so forlorn he even let me hang up his hat and coat for him. But as he entered the office I saw him squaring his shoulders. He was so used to going into that room to be belligerent that it was automatic. He growled a greeting, sat, and demanded:

"What have you got this time?"

Wolfe, lips compressed, regarded him a moment and then pointed a finger at him. "You know, Mr. Cramer, I begin to suspect I'm a jackass. Three weeks ago yesterday, when I read in the paper of Mr. Orchard's death, I should have guessed immediately why people paid him ten dollars a week. I don't mean merely the general idea of blackmail; that was an obvious possibility; I mean the whole operation, the way it was done."

"Why, have you guessed it now?"

"No. I've had it described to me."

"By whom?"

"It doesn't matter. An innocent victim. Would you like to have me describe it to you?"

"Sure. Or the other way around."

Wolfe frowned. "What? You know about it?"

"Yeah, I know about it. I do now." Cramer wasn't doing any bragging. He stayed glum. "Understand I'm saying nothing against the New York Police Department. It's the best on earth. But it's a large organization, and you can't expect everyone to know what everybody else did or is doing. My part of it is Homicide. Well. In September nineteen forty-six, nineteen months ago, a citizen lodged a complaint with a precinct detective sergeant. People had received anonymous letters about him, and he had got a phone call from a man that if he subscribed to a thing called *Track Almanac* for one year there would be no more letters. He said the stuff in the letters was lies, and he wasn't going to be swindled, and he wanted justice. Because it looked as if it might be a real job the sergeant consulted his captain. They went together to the *Track Almanac* office, found Orchard there, and jumped him. He denied it, said it must have been someone trying to queer him. The citizen listened to Orchard's voice, both direct and on the phone, and said it hadn't been his voice on the phone, it must have been a confederate. But no lead to a confederate could be found. Nothing could be found. Orchard stood pat. He refused to let them see his subscription list, on the ground that he didn't want his customers pestered, which was within his rights in the absence of a charge. The citizen's lawyer wouldn't let him swear a warrant. There were no more anonymous letters."

"Beautiful," Wolfe murmured.

"What the hell is so beautiful?"

"Excuse me. And?"

"And nothing. The captain is now retired, living on a farm in Rhode Island. The sergeant is still a sergeant, as he should be, since apparently he doesn't read the papers. He's up in a Bronx precinct, specializing in kids that throw stones at trains. Just day before yesterday the name Orchard reminded him of something! So I've got that. I've put men onto the other Orchard subscribers that we know about, except the one that was just a sucker—plenty of men to cover anybody at all close to them, to ask about anonymous letters. There have been no results on Savarese or Madeline Fraser, but we've uncovered it on the Leconne woman, the one that runs a beauty parlor. It was the same routine—the letters and the phone call, and she fell for it. She says the letters were lies, and it looks like they were, but she paid up to get them stopped, and she pushed us off, and you too, because she didn't want a stink."

Cramer made a gesture. "Does that describe it?"

"Perfectly," Wolfe granted.

"Okay. You called me, and I came because I swear to God I don't see what it gets me. It was you who got brilliant and made it that the poison was for the Fraser woman, not Orchard. Now that looks crazy, but what don't? If it was for

111

Orchard after all, who and why in that bunch? And what about Beula Poole? Were she and Orchard teaming it? Or was she horning in on his list? By God, I never saw anything like it! Have you been giving me a runaround? I want to know!"

Cramer pulled a cigar from his pocket and got his teeth closed on it.

Wolfe shook his head. "Not I," he declared. "I'm a little dizzy myself. Your description was sketchy, and it might help to fill it in. Are you in a hurry?"

"Hell no."

"Then look at this. It is important, if we are to see clearly the connection of the two events, to know exactly what the roles of Mr. Orchard and Miss Poole were. Let us say that I am an ingenious and ruthless man, and I decide to make some money by blackmailing wholesale, with little or no risk to myself."

"Orchard got poisoned," Cramer growled, "and she got shot."

"Yes," Wolfe agreed, "but I didn't. I either know people I can use or I know how to find them. I am a patient and resourceful man. I supply Orchard with funds to begin publication of *Track Almanac*. I have lists prepared, with the greatest care, of persons with ample incomes from a business or profession or job that would make them sensitive to my attack. Then I start operating. The phone calls are made neither by Orchard nor by me. Of course Orchard, who is in an exposed position, has never met me, doesn't know who I am, and probably isn't even aware that I exist. Indeed, of those engaged in the operation, very few know that I exist, possibly only one."

Wolfe rubbed his palms together. "All this is passably clever. I am taking from my victims only a small fraction of their income, and I am not threatening them with exposure of a fearful secret. Even if I knew their secrets, which I don't, I would prefer not to use them in the anonymous letters; that would not merely harass them, it would fill them with terror, and I don't want terror, I only want money. Therefore, while my lists are carefully compiled, no great amount of research is required, just enough to get only the kind of people who would be least likely to put up a fight, either by going to the police or by any other method. Even should one resort to the police, what will happen? You have already answered that, Mr. Cramer, by telling what did happen."

"That sergeant was dumb as hell," Cramer grumbled.

"Oh, no. There was the captain too. Take an hour sometime to consider what you would have done and see where you come out. What if one or two more citizens had made the same complaint? Mr. Orchard would have insisted that he was being persecuted by an enemy. In the extreme case of an avalanche of complaints, most improbable, or of an exposure by an exceptionally capable policeman, what then? Mr. Orchard would be done for, but I wouldn't. Even if he wanted to squeal, he couldn't, not on me, for he doesn't know me."

"He has been getting money to you," Cramer objected.

"Not to me. He never gets within ten miles of me. The handling of the money is an important detail and you may be sure it has been well organized. Only one man ever gets close enough to me to bring me money. It shouldn't take me long to build up a fine list of subscribers to *Track Almanac*—certainly a hundred, possibly five hundred. Let us be moderate and say two hundred. That's two thousand dollars a week. If Mr. Orchard keeps half, he can pay all expenses and have well over thirty thousand a year for his net. If he has any sense, and he has been carefully chosen and is under surveillance, that will satisfy him. For me, it's a question of my total volume. How many units do I have? New York is big enough for four or five, Chicago for two or three, Detroit, Philadelphia, and Los Angeles for two each, at least a dozen cities for one. If I wanted to stretch it I could easily get twenty units working. But we'll be moderate again and stop at twelve. That would bring me in six hundred thousand dollars a year for my share. My operating costs shouldn't be more than half that; and when you consider that my net is really net, with no income tax to pay, I am doing very well indeed."

Cramer started to say something, but Wolfe put up a hand:

"Please. As I said, all that is fairly clever, especially the avoidance of real threats about real secrets, but what makes it a masterpiece is the limitation of the tribute. All blackmailers will promise that this time is the last, but I not only make the promise, I keep it. I have an inviolable rule never to ask for a subscription renewal."

"You can't prove it."

"No, I can't. But I confidently assume it, because it is the essence, the great beauty, of the plan. A man can put up with a pain—and this was not really a pain, merely a discomfort, for people with good incomes—if he thinks he knows when it will stop, and if it stops when the time comes. But if I make them pay year after year, with no end in sight, I invite sure disaster. I'm too good a businessman for that. It is much cheaper and safer to get four new subscribers a week for each unit; that's all that is needed to keep it at a constant two hundred subscribers."

Wolfe nodded emphatically. "By all means, then, if I am to stay in business indefinitely, and I intend to, I must make that rule and rigidly adhere to it; and I do so. There will of course be many little difficulties, as there are in any enterprise, and I must also be prepared for an unforeseen contingency. For example, Mr. Orchard may get killed. If so I must know of it at once, and I must have a man in readiness to remove all papers from his office, even though there is nothing there that could possibly lead to me. I would prefer to have no inkling of the nature and extent of my operations reach unfriendly parties. But I am not panicky; why should I be? Within two weeks one of my associates—the one who makes the phone calls for my units that are managed by females—begins phoning the *Track Almanac* subscribers to tell them that their remaining payments should be made to another publication called *What to Expect*. It would have been better to discard my *Track Almanac* list and take my loss, but I don't know that. I only find it out when Miss Poole also gets killed. Luckily my surveillance is excellent. Again an office must be cleaned out, and this time under hazardous conditions and with dispatch. Quite likely my man has seen the murderer, and can even name him; but I'm not interested in catching a murderer; what I want is to save my business from these confounded interruptions. I discard both those cursed lists, destroy them, burn them, and start plans for two entirely new units. How about a weekly sheet giving the latest shopping information? Or a course in languages, any language? There are numberless possibilities."

Wolfe leaned back. "There's your connection, Mr. Cramer."

"The hell it is," Cramer mumbled. He was rubbing the side of his nose with his forefinger. He was sorting things out. After a moment he went on, "I thought maybe you were going to end up by killing both of them yourself. That would be a connection too, wouldn't it?"

"Not a very plausible one. Why would I choose that time and place and method for killing Mr. Orchard? Or even

Miss Poole—why there in her office? It wouldn't be like me. If they had to be disposed of surely I would have made better arrangements than that."

"Then you're saying it was a subscriber."

"I make the suggestion. Not necessarily a subscriber, but one who looked at things from the subscriber's viewpoint."

"Then the poison was intended for Orchard after all."

"I suppose so, confound it. I admit that's hard to swallow. It's sticking in my throat."

"Mine too." Cramer was skeptical. "One thing you overlooked. You were so interested in pretending it was you, you didn't mention who it really is. This patient ruthless bird that's pulling down over half a million a year. Could I have his name and address?"

"Not from me," Wolfe said positively. "I strongly doubt if you could finish him, and if you tried he would know who had named him. Then I would have to undertake it, and I don't want to tackle him. I work for money, to make a living, not just to keep myself alive. I don't want to be reduced to that primitive extremity."

"Nuts. You've been telling me a dream you had. You can't stand it for anyone to think you don't know everything, so you even have the brass to tell me to my face that you know his name. You don't even know he exists, any more than Orchard did."

"Oh, yes I do. I'm much more intelligent than Mr. Orchard."

"Have it your way," Cramer conceded generously. "You trade orchids with him. So what? He's not in my department. If he wasn't behind these murders I don't want him. My job is homicide. Say you didn't dream it, say it's just as you said, what comes next? How have I gained an inch or you either? Is that what you got me here for, to tell me about your goddam units in twelve different cities?"

"Partly. I didn't know your precinct sergeant had been reminded of something. But that wasn't all. Do you feel like telling me why Miss Koppel tried to get on an airplane?"

"Sure I feel like it, but I can't because I don't know. She says to see her sick mother. We've tried to find another reason that we like better, but no luck. She's under bond not to leave the state."

Wolfe nodded. "Nothing seems to fructify, does it? What I really wanted was to offer a suggestion. Would you like one?"

"Let me hear it."

"I hope it will appeal to you. You said that you have had men working in the circles of the Orchard subscribers you know about, and that there have been no results on Professor Savarese or Miss Fraser. You might have expected that, and probably did, since those two have given credible reasons for having subscribed. Why not shift your aim to another target? How many men are available for that sort of work?"

"As many as I want."

"Then put a dozen or more onto Miss Vance—or, rather, onto her associates. Make it thorough. Tell the men that the object is not to learn whether anonymous letters regarding Miss Vance have been received. Tell them that that much has been confidently assumed, and that their job is to find out what the letters said, and who got them and when. It will require pertinacity to the farthest limit of permissible police conduct. The man good enough actually to secure one of the letters will be immediately promoted."

Cramer sat scowling. Probably he was doing the same as me, straining for a quick but comprehensive flashback of all the things that Elinor Vance had seen or done, either in our presence or to our knowledge. Finally he inquired:

"Why her?"

Wolfe shook his head. "If I explained you would say I was telling you another dream. I assure you that in my opinion the reason is good."

"How many letters to how many people?"

Wolfe's brows went up. "My dear sir! If I knew that would I let you get a finger in it? I would have her here ready for delivery, with evidence. What the deuce is wrong with it? I am merely suggesting a specific line of inquiry on a specific person whom you have already been tormenting for over three weeks."

"You're letting my finger in now. If it's any good why don't you hire men with your clients' money and sail on through?"

Wolfe snorted. He was disgusted. "Very well," he said. "I'll do that. Don't bother about it. Doubtless your own contrivances are far superior. Another sergeant may be reminded of something that happened at the turn of the century."

Cramer stood up. I thought he was going to leave without a word, but he spoke. "That's pretty damn cheap, Wolfe. You would never have heard of that sergeant if I hadn't told you about him. Freely."

He turned and marched out. I made allowances for both of them because their nerves were on edge. After three weeks for Cramer, and more than two for Wolfe, they were no closer to the killer of Cyril Orchard than when they started.

20

I HAVE to admit that for me the toss to Elinor Vance was a passed ball. It went by me away out of reach. I halfway expected that now at last we would get some hired help, but when I asked Wolfe if I should line up Saul and Fred and Orrie he merely grunted. I wasn't much surprised, since it was in accordance with our new policy of letting the cops do it. It was a cinch that Cramer's first move on returning to his headquarters would be to start a pack sniffing for anonymous letters about Elinor Vance.

After lunch I disposed of a minor personal problem by getting Wolfe's permission to pay a debt, though that wasn't the way I put it. I told him that I would like to call Lon Cohen and give him the dope on how subscriptions to *Track Almanac* and *What to Expect* had been procured, of course without any hint of a patient ruthless master mind who didn't exist, and naming no names. My arguments were (a) that Wolfe had fished it up himself and therefore Cramer had no copyright, (b) that it was desirable to have a newspaper under an obligation, (c) that it would serve them right for the vicious editorial they had run, and (d) that it might possibly start a fire somewhere that would give us a smoke signal. Wolfe nodded, but I waited until he had gone up to the plant rooms to phone Lon to pay up. If I had done it in his hearing he's so damn suspicious that some word, or a shade of a tone, might have started him asking questions.

Another proposal I made later on didn't do so well. He turned it down flat. Since it was to be assumed that I had forgotten the name Arnold Zeck, I used Duncan instead. I reminded Wolfe that he had told Cramer that it was likely that an employee of Duncan's had seen the killer of Beula Poole, and could even name him. What I proposed was to call the Midland number and leave a message for Duncan to phone Wolfe. If and when he did so Wolfe would make an offer: if Duncan would come through on the killer, not for quotation of course, Wolfe would agree to forget that he had ever heard tell of anyone whose name began with Z—pardon me, D.

All I got was my head snapped off. First, Wolfe would make no such bargain with a criminal, especially a dysgenic one; and second, there would be no further communication between him and that nameless buzzard unless the buzzard started it. That seemed shortsighted to me. If he didn't intend to square off with the bird unless he had to, why not take what he could get? After dinner that evening I tried to bring it up again, but he wouldn't discuss it.

The following morning, Friday, we had a pair of visitors that we hadn't seen for quite a while: Walter B. Anderson, the Hi-Spot president, and Fred Owen, the director of public relations. When the doorbell rang a little before noon and I went to the front and saw them on the stoop, my attitude was quite different from what it had been the first time. They had no photographers along, and they were clients in good standing entitled to one hell of a beef if they only knew it, and there was a faint chance that they had a concealed weapon, maybe a hatpin, to stick into Wolfe. So without going to the office to check I welcomed them across the threshold.

Wolfe greeted them without any visible signs of rapture, but at least he didn't grump. He even asked them how they did. While they were getting seated he shifted in his chair so he could give his eyes to either one without excessive exertion for his neck muscles. He actually apologized:

"It isn't astonishing if you gentlemen are getting a little impatient. But if you are exasperated, so am I. I had no idea it would drag on like this. No murderer likes to be caught, naturally; but this one seems to have an extraordinary aversion to it. Would you like me to describe what has been accomplished?"

"We know pretty well," Owen stated. He was wearing a dark brown double-breasted pin-stripe that must have taken at least five fittings to get it the way it looked.

"We know too well," the president corrected him. Usually I am tolerant of the red-faced plump type, but every time that geezer opened his mouth I wanted to shut it and not by talking.

Wolfe frowned. "I've admitted your right to exasperation. You needn't insist on it."

"We're not exasperated with you, Mr. Wolfe," Owen declared.

"I am," the president corrected him again. "With the whole damn thing and everything and everyone connected with it. For a while I've been willing to string along with the idea that there can't be any argument against a Hooper in the high twenties, but I've thought I might be wrong and now I know I was. My God, blackmail! Were you responsible for that piece in the *Gazette* this morning?"

"Well . . ." Wolfe was being judicious. "I would say that the responsibility rests with the man who conceived the scheme. I discovered and disclosed it—"

"It doesn't matter." Anderson waved it aside. "What does matter is that my company and my product cannot and will not be connected in the public mind with blackmail. That's dirty. That makes people gag."

"I absolutely agree," Owen asserted.

"Murder is moderately dirty too," Wolfe objected.

"No," Anderson said flatly. "Murder is sensational and exciting, but it's not like blackmail and anonymous letters. I'm through. I've had enough of it."

He got a hand in his breast pocket and pulled out an envelope, from which he extracted an oblong strip of blue paper. "Here's a check for your fee, the total amount. I can collect from the others—or not. I'll see. Send me a bill for expenses to date. You understand, I'm calling it off."

Owen had got up to take the check and hand it to Wolfe. Wolfe took a squint at it and let it drop to the desk.

"Indeed." Wolfe picked up the check, gave it another look, and dropped it again. "Have you consulted the other parties to our arrangement?"

"No, and I don't intend to. What do you care? That's the full amount, isn't it?"

"Yes, the amount's all right. But why this headlong retreat? What has suddenly scared you so?"

"Nothing has scared me." Anderson came forward in his chair. "Look, Wolfe. I came down here myself to make sure there's no slip-up on this. The deal is off, beginning right now. If you listened to the Fraser program this morning you didn't hear my product mentioned. I'm paying that off too, and clearing out. If you think I'm scared you don't know me. I don't scare. But I know how to take action when the circumstances require it, and that's what I'm doing."

He left his chair, leaned over Wolfe's desk, stretched a short fat arm, and tapped the check with a short stubby forefinger. "I'm no welcher! I'll pay your expenses just like I'm paying this! I'm not blaming you, to hell with that, but from this minute—you—are—not—working—for—me!"

With the last six words the finger jabbed the desk, at the rate of about three jabs to a word.

"Come on Fred," the president commanded, and the pair tramped out to the hall.

I moseyed over as far as the office door to see that they didn't make off with my new twenty-dollar gray spring hat, and, when they were definitely gone, returned to my desk, sat, and commented to Wolfe:

"He seems to be upset."

"Take a letter to him."

I got my notebook and pen. Wolfe cleared his throat.

"Not dear Mr. Anderson, dear sir. Regarding our conversation at my office this morning, I am engaged with others as well as you, and, since my fee is contingent upon a performance, I am obliged to continue until the performance is completed. The check you gave me will be held in my safe until that time."

I looked up. "Sincerely?"

"I suppose so. There's nothing insincere about it. When you go out to mail it go first to the bank and have the check certified."

"That shifts the contingency," I remarked, opening the drawer where I kept letterheads, "to whether the bank stays solvent or not."

It was at that moment, the moment when I was putting the paper in the typewriter, that Wolfe really settled down to work on the Orchard case. He leaned back, shut his eyes, and began exercising his lips. He was like that when I left on my errand, and still like that when I got back. At such times I don't have to tiptoe or keep from rustling papers; I can bang the typewriter or make phone calls or use the vacuum cleaner and he doesn't hear it.

All the rest of that day and evening, up till bedtime, except for intermissions for meals and the afternoon conclave in the plant rooms, he kept at it, with no word or sign to give me a hint what kind of trail he had found, if any. In a way it was perfectly jake with me, for at least it showed that he had decided we would do our own cooking, but in another way it wasn't so hot. When it goes on hour after hour, as it did that Friday, the chances are that he's finding himself just about cornered, and there's no telling how desperate he'll be when he picks a hole to bust out through. A couple of years ago, after spending most of a day figuring one out, he ended up with a charade that damn near got nine human beings asphyxiated with ciphogene, including him and me, not to mention Inspector Cramer.

When both the clock and my wrist watch said it was close to midnight, and there he still was, I inquired politely:

"Shall we have some coffee to keep awake?"

His mutter barely reached me: "Go to bed."

I did so.

21

I NEEDN'T have worried. He did give birth, but not to one of his fantastic freaks. The next morning, Saturday, when Fritz returned to the kitchen after taking up the breakfast tray he told me I was wanted.

Since Wolfe likes plenty of air at night but a good warm room at breakfast time it had been necessary, long ago, to install a contraption that would automatically close his window at 6:00 A.M. As a result the eight o'clock temperature permits him to have his tray on a table near the window without bothering to put on a dressing gown. Seated there, his hair not yet combed, his feet bare, and all the yardage of his yellow pajamas dazzling in the morning sun, he is something to blink at, and it's too bad that Fritz and I are the only ones who ever have the privilege.

I told him it was a nice morning, and he grunted. He will not admit that a morning is bearable, let alone nice, until, having had his second cup of coffee, he has got himself fully dressed.

"Instructions," he growled.

I sat down, opened my notebook, and uncapped my pen. He instructed:

"Get some ordinary plain white paper of a cheap grade; I doubt if any of ours will do. Say five by eight. Type this on it, single-spaced, no date or salutation."

He shut his eyes. "Since you are a friend of Elinor Vance, this is something you should know. During her last year at college the death of a certain person was ascribed to natural causes and was never properly investigated. Another incident that was never investigated was the disappearance of a jar of cyanide from the electroplating shop of Miss Vance's brother. It would be interesting to know if there was any connection between those two incidents. Possibly an inquiry into both of them would suggest such a connection."

"That all?"

"Yes. No signature. No envelope. Fold the paper and soil it a little; give it the appearance of having been handled. This is Saturday, but an item in the morning paper tells of the withdrawal of Hi-Spot from sponsorship of Miss Fraser's program, so I doubt if those people will have gone off for week ends. You may even find that they are together, conferring; that would suit our purpose best. But either together or singly, see them; show them the anonymous letter, ask if they have ever seen it or one similar to it; be insistent and as pestiferous as possible."

"Including Miss Vance herself?"

"Let circumstances decide. If they are together and she is with them, yes. Presumably she has already been alerted by Mr. Cramer's men."

"The professor? Savarese?"

"No, don't bother with him." Wolfe drank coffee. "That's all."

I stood up. "I might get more or better results if I knew what we're after. Are we expecting Elinor Vance to break down and confess? Or am I nagging one of them into pulling a gun on me, or what?"

I should have known better, with him still in his pajamas and his hair tousled.

"You're following instructions," he said peevishly. "If I knew what you're going to get I wouldn't have had to resort to this shabby stratagem."

"Shabby is right," I agreed, and left him.

I would of course obey orders, for the same reason that a good soldier does, namely he'd better, but I was not filled with enough zeal to make me hurry my breakfast. My attitude as I set about the preliminaries of the operation was that if this was the best he could do he might as well have stayed dormant. I did not believe that he had anything on Elinor Vance. He does sometimes hire Saul or Orrie or Fred without letting me know what they're up to or, more rarely, even that they're working for him, but I can always tell by seeing if money has been taken from the safe. The money was all present or accounted for. You can judge my frame of mind when I state that I halfway suspected that he had picked on Elinor merely because I had gone to a little trouble to have her seated nearest to me the night of the party.

He was, however, right about the week ends. I didn't start on the phone calls until nine-thirty, not wanting to get them out of bed for something which I regarded as about as useful as throwing rocks at the moon. The first one I tried, Bill Meadows, said he hadn't had breakfast yet and he didn't know when he would have some free time, because he was due at Miss Fraser's apartment at eleven for a conference and there was no telling how long it would last. That indicated that I would have a chance to throw at two or more moons with one stone, and another couple of phone calls verified it. There was a meeting on. I did the morning chores, buzzed the plant rooms to inform Wolfe, and left a little before eleven and headed uptown.

To show you what a murder case will do to people's lives, the password routine had been abandoned. But it by no means followed that it was easier than it had been to get up to apartment 10B. Quite the contrary. Evidently journalists and others had been trying all kinds of dodges to get a ride in the elevator, for the distinguished-looking hallman wasn't a particle interested in what I said my name was, and he steeled himself to betray no sign of recognition. He simply used the phone, and in a few minutes Bill Meadows emerged from the elevator and walked over to us. We said hello.

"Strong said you'd probably show up," he said. Neither his tone nor his expression indicated that they had been pacing up and down waiting for me. "Miss Fraser wants to know if it's something urgent."

"Mr. Wolfe thinks it is."

"All right, come on."

He was so preoccupied that he went into the elevator first.

I decided that if he tried leaving me alone in the enormous living room with the assorted furniture, to wait until I was summoned, I would just stick to his heels, but that proved to be unnecessary. He couldn't have left me alone there because that was where they were.

Madeline Fraser was on the green burlap divan, propped against a dozen cushions. Deborah Koppel was seated on the piano bench. Elinor Vance perched on a corner of the massive old black walnut table. Tully Strong had the edge of his sitter on the edge of the pink silk chair, and Nat

123

Traub was standing. That was all as billed, but there was an added attraction. Also standing, at the far end of the long divan, was Nancylee Shepherd.

"It was Goodwin," Bill Meadows told them, but they would probably have deduced it anyhow, since I had dropped my hat and coat in the hall and was practically at his elbow. He spoke to Miss Fraser:

"He says it's something urgent."

Miss Fraser asked me briskly, "Will it take long, Mr. Goodwin?" She looked clean and competent, as if she had had a good night's sleep, a shower, a healthy vigorous rub, and a thorough breakfast.

I told her I was afraid it might.

"Then I'll have to ask you to wait." She was asking a favor. She certainly had the knack of being personal without making you want to back off. "Mr. Traub has to leave soon for an appointment, and we have to make an important decision. You know, of course, that we have lost a sponsor. I suppose I ought to feel low about it, but I really don't. Do you know how many firms we have had offers from, to take the Hi-Spot place? Sixteen!"

"Wonderful!" I admired. "Sure, I'll wait." I crossed to occupy a chair outside the conference zone.

They forgot, immediately and completely, that I was there. All but one: Nancylee. She changed position so she could keep her eyes on me, and her expression showed plainly that she considered me tricky, ratty, and unworthy of trust.

"We've got to start eliminating," Tully Strong declared. He had his spectacles off, holding them in his hand. "As I understand it there are just five serious contenders."

"Four," Elinor Vance said, glancing at a paper she held. "I've crossed off Fluff, the biscuit dough. You said to, didn't you, Lina?"

"It's a good company," Traub said regretfully. "One of the best. Their radio budget is over three million."

"You're just making it harder, Nat," Deborah Koppel told him. "We can't take all of them. I thought your favorite was Meltettes."

"It is," Traub agreed, "but these are all very fine accounts. What do you think of Meltettes, Miss Fraser?" He was the only one of the bunch who didn't call her Lina.

"I haven't tried them." She glanced around. "Where are they?"

Nancylee, apparently not so concentrated on me as to

124

miss any word or gesture of her idol, spoke up: "There on the piano, Miss Fraser. Do you want them?"

"We have got to eliminate," Strong insisted, stabbing the air with his spectacles for emphasis. "I must repeat, as representative of the other sponsors, that they are firmly and unanimously opposed to Sparkle, if it is to be served on the program as Hi-Spot was. They never liked the idea and they don't want it resumed."

"It's already crossed off," Elinor Vance stated. "With Fluff and Sparkle out, that leaves four."

"Not on account of the sponsors," Miss Fraser put in. "We just happen to agree with them. They aren't going to decide this. We are."

"You mean you are, Lina." Bill Meadows sounded a little irritated. "What the hell, we all know that. You don't want Fluff because Cora made some biscuits and you didn't like 'em. You don't want Sparkle because they want it served on the program, and God knows I don't blame you."

Elinor Vance repeated, "That leaves four."

"All right, eliminate!" Strong persisted.

"We're right where we were before," Deborah Koppel told them. "The trouble is, there's no real objection to any of the four, and I think Bill's right, I think we have to put it up to Lina."

"I am prepared," Nat Traub announced, in the tone of a man burning bridges, "to say that I will vote for Meltettes."

For my part, I was prepared to say that I would vote for nobody. Sitting there taking them in, as far as I could tell the only strain they were under was the pressure of picking the right sponsor. If, combined with that, one of them was contending with the nervous wear and tear of a couple of murders, he was too good for me. As the argument got warmer it began to appear that, though they were agreed that the final word was up to Miss Fraser, each of them had a favorite among the four entries left. That was what complicated the elimination.

Naturally, on account of the slip of paper I had in my pocket, I was especially interested in Elinor Vance, but the sponsor problem seemed to be monopolizing her attention as completely as that of the others. I would of course have to follow instructions and proceed with my errand as soon as they gave me a chance, but I was beginning to feel silly. While Wolfe had left it pretty vague, one thing was plain, that I was supposed to give them a severe jolt, and I doubted if I had what it would take. When they got worked up to

the point of naming the winner—settling on the lucky product that would be cast for the role sixteen had applied for
—bringing up the subject of an anonymous letter, even one
implying that one of them was a chronic murderer, would
be an anticlimax. With a serious problem like that just trium-
phantly solved, what would they care about a little thing
like murder?

But I was dead wrong. I found that out incidentally, as
a by-product of their argument. It appeared that two of the
contenders were deadly rivals, both clawing for children's
dimes: a candy bar called Happy Andy and a little box of
tasty delights called Meltettes. It was the later that Traub
had decided to back unequivocally, and he, when the question came to a head which of those two to eliminate, again
asked Miss Fraser if she had tried Meltettes. She told him no.
He asked if she had tried Happy Andy. She said yes. Then,
he insisted, it was only fair for her to try Meltettes.

"All right," she agreed. "There on the piano, Debby, that
little red box. Toss it over."

"No!" a shrill voice cried. It was Nancylee. Everyone
looked at her. Deborah Koppel, who had picked up the little
red cardboard box, asked her:

"What's the matter?"

"It's dangerous!" Nancylee was there, a hand outstretched.
"Give it to me. I'll eat one first!"

It was only a romantic kid being dramatic, and all she
rated from that bunch, if I had read their pulses right, was
a laugh and a brush-off, but that was what showed me I had
been dead wrong. There wasn't even a snicker. No one said
a word. They all froze, staring at Nancylee, with only one
exception. That was Deborah Koppel. She held the box away
from Nancylee's reaching hand and told her contemp-
tuously:

"Don't be silly."

"I mean it!" the girl cried. "Let me—"

"Nonsense." Deborah pushed her back, opened the flap of
the box, took out an object, popped it into her mouth,
chewed once or twice, swallowed, and then spat explosive-
ly, ejecting a spray of little particles.

I was the first, by maybe a tenth of a second, to realize
that there was something doing. It wasn't so much the spitting, for that could conceivably have been merely her way
of voting against Meltettes, as it was the swift terrible con-
tortion of her features. As I bounded across to her she left

the piano bench with a spasmodic jerk, got erect with her hands flung high, and screamed:

"Lina! Don't! Don't let—"

I was at her, with a hand on her arm, and Bill Meadows was there too, but her muscles all in convulsion took us along as she fought toward the divan, and Madeline Fraser was there to meet her and get supporting arms around her. But somehow the three of us together failed to hold her up or get her onto the divan. She went down until her knees were on the floor, with one arm stretched rigid across the burlap of the divan, and would have gone the rest of the way but for Miss Fraser, also on her knees.

I straightened, wheeled, and told Nat Traub: "Get a doctor quick." I saw Nancylee reaching to pick up the little red cardboard box and snapped at her: "Let that alone and behave yourself." Then to the rest of them: "Let everything alone, hear me?"

22

AROUND four o'clock I could have got permission to go home if I had insisted, but it seemed better to stay as long as there was a chance of picking up another item for my report. I had already phoned Wolfe to explain why I wasn't following his instructions.

All of those who had been present at the conference were still there, very much so, except Deborah Koppel, who had been removed in a basket when several gangs of city scientists had finished their part of it. She had been dead when the doctor arrived. The others were still alive but not in a mood to brag about it.

At four o'clock Lieutenant Rowcliff and an assistant D.A. were sitting on the green burlap divan, arguing whether the taste of cyanide should warn people in time to refrain from swallowing. That seemed pointless, since whether it should or not it usually doesn't, and anyway the only ones who could qualify as experts are those who have tried it, and none of them is available. I moved on. At the big oak table another lieutenant was conversing with Bill Meadows, meanwhile referring to notes on loose sheets of paper. I went on by. In the dining room a sergeant and a private were pecking away at Elinor Vance. I passed through. In the kitchen a dick with a pug nose was holding a sheet of paper, one of a series, flat on the table while Cora, the female wrestler, put her initials on it.

Turning and going back the way I had come, I continued on to the square hall, opened a door at its far end, and went through. This, the room without a name, was more densely populated than the others. Tully Strong and Nat Traub were on chairs against opposite walls. Nancylee was standing by a window. A dick was seated in the center of the room, another was leaning against a wall, and Sergeant Purley Stebbins was sort of strolling around.

That called the roll, for I knew that Madeline Fraser was in the room beyond, her bedroom, where I had first met the bunch of them, having a talk with Inspector Cramer. The way I knew that, I had just been ordered out by Deputy Commissioner O'Hara, who was in there with them.

The first series of quickies, taking them one at a time on a gallop, had been staged in the dining room by Cramer himself. Cramer and an assistant D.A. had sat at one side of the table, with the subject across from them, and me seated a little to the rear of the subject's elbow. The theory of that arrangement was that if the subject's memory showed a tendency to conflict with mine, I could tip Cramer off by sticking out my tongue or some other signal without being seen by the subject. The dick-stenographer had been at one end of the table, and other units of the personnel had hung around.

Since they were by no means strangers to Cramer and he was already intimately acquainted with their biographies, he could keep it brief and concentrate chiefly on two points; their positions and movements during the conference, and the box of Meltettes. On the former there were some contradictions on minor details, but only what you might expect under the circumstances; and I, who had been there, saw no indication that anyone was trying to fancy it up.

On the latter, the box of Meltettes, there was no contradiction at all. By noon Friday, the preceding day, the news had begun to spread that Hi-Spot was bowing out, though it had not yet been published. For some time Meltettes had been on the Fraser waiting list, to grab a vacancy if one occurred. Friday morning Nat Traub, whose agency had the Meltettes account, had phoned his client the news, and the client had rushed him a carton of its product by messenger.

A carton held forty-eight of the little red cardboard boxes. Traub, wishing to lose no time on a matter of such urgency and importance, and not wanting to lug the whole carton, had taken one little box from it and dropped it in his pocket, and hotfooted it to the FBC building, arriving at the studio just before the conclusion of the Fraser broadcast. He had spoken to Miss Fraser and Miss Koppel on behalf of Meltettes and handed the box to Miss Koppel.

Miss Koppel had passed the box on to Elinor Vance, who had put it in her bag—the same bag that had been used to transport sugared coffee in a Hi-Spot bottle. The three women had lunched in a near-by restaurant and then gone to Miss Fraser's apartment, where they had been joined later by Bill Meadows and Tully Strong for an exploratory discussion of the sponsor problem. Soon after their arrival at the apartment Elinor had taken the box of Meltettes from her bag and given it to Miss Fraser, who had put it on the big oak table in the living room.

That had been between two-thirty and three o'clock Friday afternoon, and that was as far as it went. No one knew how or when the box had been moved from the oak table to the piano. There was a blank space, completely blank, of about eighteen hours, ending around nine o'clock Saturday morning, when Cora, on a dusting mission, had seen it on the piano. She had picked it up for a swipe of the dustcloth on the piano top and put it down again. Its next appearance was two hours later, when Nancylee, soon after her arrival at the apartment, had spotted it and been tempted to help herself, even going so far as to get her clutches on it, but had been scared off when she saw that Miss Koppel's eye was on her. That, Nancylee explained, was how she had known where the box was when Miss Fraser had asked.

As you can see, it left plenty of room for inch-by-inch digging and sifting, which was lucky for everybody from privates to inspectors who are supposed to earn their pay, for there was no other place to dig at all. Relationships and motives and suspicions had already had all the juice squeezed out of them. So by four o'clock Saturday afternoon a hundred grown men, if not more, were scattered around the city, doing their damnedest to uncover another little splinter of a fact, any old fact, about that box of Meltettes. Some of them, of course, were getting results. For instance, word had come from the laboratory that the box, as it came to them, had held eleven Meltettes; that one of them, which had obviously been operated on rather skillfully, had about twelve grains of cyanide mixed into its insides; and that the other ten were quite harmless, with no sign of having been tampered with. Meltettes, they said, fitted snugly into the box in pairs, and the cyanided one had been on top, at the end of the box which opened.

And other reports, including of course fingerprints. Most of them had been relayed to Cramer in my presence. Whatever he may have thought they added up to, it looked to me very much like a repeat performance by the artist who had painted the sugared coffee picture: so many crossing lines and overlapping colors that no resemblance to any known animal or other object was discernible.

Returning to the densely populated room with no name after my tour of inspection. I made some witty remark to Purley Stebbins and lowered myself into a chair. As I said, I could probably have bulled my way out and gone home, but I didn't want to. What prospect did it offer? I would have fiddled around until Wolfe came down to the office, made my report, and then what? He would either have grunted in disgust, found something to criticize, and lowered his iron curtain again, or he would have gone into another trance and popped out around midnight with some bright idea like typing an anonymous letter about Bill Meadows flunking in algebra his last year in high school. I preferred to stick around in the faint hope that something would turn up.

And something did: I had abandoned the idea of making some sense out of the crossing lines and overlapping colors, given up trying to get a rise out of Purley, and was exchanging hostile glares with Nancylee, when the door from the square hall opened and a lady entered. She darted a glance around and told Purley Inspector Cramer had sent for her. He crossed to the far door which led to Miss Fraser's bedroom, opened it, and closed it after she had passed through.

I knew her by sight but not her name, and even had an opinion of her, namely that she was the most presentable of all the female dicks I had seen. With nothing else to do, I figured out what Cramer wanted with her, and had just come to the correct conclusion when the door opened again and I got it verified. Cramer appeared first, then Deputy Commissioner O'Hara. Cramer spoke to Purley:

"Get 'em all in here."

Purley flew to obey. Nat Traub asked wistfully, "Have you made any progress, Inspector?"

Cramer didn't even have the decency to growl at him, let alone reply. That seemed unnecessarily rude, so I told Traub:

"Yeah, they've reached an important decision. You're all going to be frisked."

It was ill-advised, especially with O'Hara there, since he has never forgiven me for being clever once, but I was frustrated and edgy. O'Hara gave me an evil look and Cramer told me to close my trap.

The others came straggling in with their escorts. I surveyed the lot and would have felt genuinely sorry for them if I had known which one to leave out. There was no question now about the kind of strain they were under, and it had nothing to do with picking a sponsor.

Cramer addressed them:

"I want to say to you people that as long as you cooperate with us we have no desire to make it any harder for you than we have to. You can't blame us for feeling we have to bear down on you, in view of the fact that all of you lied, and kept on lying, about the bottle that the stuff came out of that killed Orchard. I called you in here to tell you that we're going to search your persons. The position is this, we would be justified in taking you all down and booking you as material witnesses, and that's what we'll do if any of you object to the search. Miss Fraser made no objection. A policewoman is in there with her now. The women will be taken in there one at a time. The men will be taken by Lieutenant Rowcliff and Sergeant Stebbins, also one at a time, to another room. Does anyone object?"

It was pitiful. They were in no condition to object, even if he had announced his intention of having clusters of Meltettes tattooed on their chests. Nobody made a sound except Nancylee, who merely shrilled:

"Oh, I never!"

I crossed my legs and prepared to sit it out. And so I did, up to a point. Purley and Rowcliff took Tully Strong first. Soon the female dick appeared and got Elinor Vance. Evidently they were being thorough, for it was a good eight minutes before Purley came back with Strong and took Bill Meadows, and the lady took just as long with Elinor Vance. The last two on the list were Nancylee in one direction and Nat Traub in the other.

That is, they were the last two as I had it. But when Rowcliff and Purley returned with Traub and handed Cramer some slips of paper, O'Hara barked at them:

"What about Goodwin?"

"Oh, him?" Rowcliff asked.

"Certainly him! He was here, wasn't he?"

Rowcliff looked at Cramer. Cramer looked at me.

I grinned at O'Hara. "What if I object, Commissioner?"

"Try it! That won't help you any!"

"The hell it won't. It will either preserve my dignity or start a string of firecrackers. What do you want to bet my big brother can't lick your big brother?"

He took a step toward me. "You resist, do you?"

"You're damn right I do." My hand did a half circle. "Before twenty witnesses."

He wheeled. "Send him down, Inspector. To my office. Charge him. Then have him searched."

"Yes, sir." Cramer was frowning. "First, would you mind stepping into another room with me? Perhaps I haven't fully explained the situation—"

"I understand it perfectly! Wolfe has cooperated, so you say—to what purpose? What has happened? Another murder! Wolfe has got you all buffaloed, and I'm sick and tired of it! Take him to my office!"

"No one has got me buffaloed," Cramer rasped. "Take him, Purley. I'll phone about a charge."

23

THERE were two things I liked about Deputy Commissioner O'Hara's office. First, it was there that I had been clever on a previous occasion, and therefore it aroused agreeable memories, and second, I like nice surroundings and it was the most attractive room at Centre Street, being on a corner with six large windows, and furnished with chairs and rugs and other items which had been paid for by O'Hara's rich wife.

I sat at ease in one of the comfortable chairs. The contents of my pockets were stacked in a neat pile on a corner of O'Hara's big shiny mahogany desk, except for one item which Purley Stebbins had in his paw. Purley was so mad his face was a red sunset, and he was stuttering.

"Don't be a g-goddam fool," he exhorted me. "If you clam it with O'Hara when he gets here he'll jug you sure as hell, and it's after six o'clock so where'll you spend the night?" He shook his paw at me, the one holding the item taken from my pocket. "Tell me about this!"

I shook my head firmly. "You know, Purley," I said without rancor, "this is pretty damn ironic. You frisked that bunch of suspects and got nothing at all—I could tell that from the way you and Rowcliff looked. But on me, absolutely innocent of wrongdoing, you find what you think is an incriminating document. So here I am, sunk, facing God knows what kind of doom. I try to catch a glimpse of the future, and what do I see?"

"Oh, shut up!"

"No, I've got to talk to someone." I glanced at my wrist. "As you say, it's after six o'clock. Mr. Wolfe has come down from the plant rooms, expecting to find me awaiting him in the office, ready for my report of the day's events. He'll be disappointed. You know how he'll feel. Better still, you know what he'll do. He'll be so frantic he'll start looking up numbers and dialing them himself. I am offering ten to one that he has already called the Fraser apartment and spoken to Cramer. How much of it do you want? A dime? A buck?"

"Can it, you goddam ape." Purley was resigning. "Save it for O'Hara, he'll be here pretty soon. I hope they give you a cell with bedbugs."

"I would prefer," I said courteously, "to chat."

"Then chat about this."

"No. For the hundredth time, no. I detest anonymous letters and I don't like to talk about them."

He went to a chair and sat facing me. I got up, crossed to bookshelves, selected CRIME AND CRIMINALS, by Mercier, and returned to my seat with it.

Purley had been wrong. O'Hara was not there pretty soon. When I glanced at my wrist every ten minutes or so I did it on the sly because I didn't want Purley to think I was getting impatient. It was a little past seven when I looked up from my book at the sound of a buzzer. Purley went to a phone on the desk and had a talk with it. He hung up, returned to his chair, sat, and after a moment spoke:

"That was the Deputy Commissioner. He is going to have his dinner. I'm to keep you here till he comes."

"Good," I said approvingly. "This is a fascinating book."

"He thinks you're boiling. You bastard."

I shrugged.

I kept my temper perfectly for another hour or more, and then, still there with my book, I became aware that I was starting to lose control. The trouble was that I had begun to feel hungry, and that was making me sore. Then there was another factor: what the hell was Wolfe doing? That, I admit, was unreasonable. Any phoning he did would be to Cramer or O'Hara, or possibly someone at the D.A.'s office, and with me cooped up as I was I wouldn't hear even an echo. If he had learned where I was and tried to get me, they wouldn't have put him through, since Purley had orders from O'Hara that I was to make no calls. But what with feeling hungry and getting no word from the outside world, I became aware that I was beginning to be offended, and that would not do. I forced my mind away from food and other aggravating aspects, including the number of revolutions the minute hand of my watch had made, and turned another page.

It was ten minutes to nine when the door opened and O'Hara and Cramer walked in. Purley stood up. I was in the middle of a paragraph and so merely flicked one eye enough to see who it was. O'Hara hung his hat and coat on a rack, and Cramer dropped his on a chair. O'Hara strode to his desk, crossing my bow so close that I could easily have tripped him by stretching a leg.

Cramer looked tired. Without spending a glance on me he nodded at Purley.

"Has he opened up?"

"No, sir. Here it is." Purley handed him the item.

They had both had it read to them on the phone, but they wanted to see it. Cramer read it through twice and then handed it to O'Hara. While that was going on I went to the shelves and replaced the book, had a good stretch and yawn, and returned to my chair.

Cramer glared down at me. "What have you got to say?"

"More of the same," I told him. "I've explained to the sergeant, who has had nothing to eat by the way, that that thing has no connection whatever with any murder or any other crime, and therefore questions about it are out of order."

"You've been charged as a material witness."

"Yeah, I know, Purley showed it to me. Why don't you ask Mr. Wolfe? He might be feeling generous."

"The hell he might. We have. Look, Goodwin—"

"I'll handle him, Inspector." O'Hara speaking. He was an

energetic cuss. He had gone clear around his desk to sit down, but now he arose and came clear around it again to confront me, I looked up at him inquiringly, not a bit angry.

He was trying to control himself. "You can't possibly get away with it," he stated. "It's incredible that you have the gall to try it, both you and Wolfe. Anonymous letters are a central factor in this case, a vital factor. You went up to that apartment today to see those people, and you had in your pocket an anonymous letter about one of them, practically accusing her of murder. Do you mean to tell me that you take the position that that letter has no connection with the crimes under investigation?"

"I sure do. Evidently Mr. Wolfe does too." I made a gesture. "Corroboration."

"You take and maintain that position while aware of the penalty that may be imposed upon conviction for an obstruction of justice?"

"I do."

O'Hara turned and blurted at Cramer, "Get Wolfe down here! Damn it, we should have hauled him in hours ago!"

This, I thought to myself, is something like. Now we ought to see some fur fly.

But we didn't, at least not as O'Hara had it programed. What interfered was a phone call. The buzzer sounded, and Purley, seeing that his superiors were too worked up to hear it, went to the desk and answered. After a word he told Cramer, "For you, Inspector," and Cramer crossed and got it. O'Hara stood glaring down at me, but, having his attention called by a certain tone taken by Cramer's voice, turned to look that way. Finally Cramer hung up. The expression on his face was that of a man trying to decide what it was he just swallowed.

"Well?" O'Hara demanded.

"The desk just had a call," Cramer said, "from the WPIT newsroom. WPIT is doing the script for the ten o'clock newscast, and they're including an announcement received a few minutes ago from Nero Wolfe. Wolfe announces that he has solved the murder cases, all three of them, with no assistance from the police, and that very soon, probably sometime tomorrow, he will be ready to tell the District Attorney the name of the murderer and to furnish all necessary information. WPIT wants to know if we have any comment."

Of course it was vulgar, but I couldn't help it. I threw

back my head and let out a roar. It wasn't so much the news itself as it was the look on O'Hara's face as the full beauty of it seeped through to him.

"The fat bum!" Purley whimpered.

I told O'Hara distinctly: "The next time Cramer asks you to step into another room with him I'd advise you to step."

He didn't hear me.

"It wasn't a question," Cramer said, "of Wolfe having me buffaloed. With him the only question is what has he got and how and when will he use it. If that goes on the air I would just as soon quit."

"What—" O'Hara stopped to wet his lips. "What would you suggest?"

Cramer didn't answer. He pulled a cigar from his pocket, slow motion, got it between his teeth, took it out again and hurled it for the wastebasket, missing by two feet, walked to a chair, sat down, and breathed.

"There are only two things," he said. "Just let it land is one. The other is to ask Goodwin to call him and request him to recall the announcement—and tell him he'll be home right away to report." Cramer breathed again. "I won't ask Goodwin that. Do you want to?"

"No! It's blackmail!" O'Hara yelled in pain.

"Yeah," Cramer agreed. "Only when Wolfe does it there's nothing anonymous about it. The newscast will be on in thirty-five minutes."

O'Hara would rather have eaten soap. "It may be a bluff," he pleaded. "Pure bluff!"

"Certainly it may. And it may not. It's easy enough to call it—just sit down and wait. If you're not going to call on Goodwin I guess I'll have to see if I can get hold of the Commissioner." Cramer stood up.

O'Hara turned to me. I have to hand it to him, he looked me in the eye as he asked:

"Will you do it?"

I grinned at him. "That warrant Purley showed me is around somewhere. It will be vacated?"

"Yes."

"Okay, I've got witnesses." I crossed to the desk and began returning my belongings to the proper pockets. The anonymous letter was there where O'Hara had left it when he had advanced to overwhelm me, and I picked it up and displayed it. "I'm taking this," I said, "but I'll let you look at it again if you want to. May I use the phone?"

I circled the desk, dropped into O'Hara's personal chair, pulled the instruments to me, and asked the male switchboard voice to get Mr. Nero Wolfe. The voice asked who I was and I told it. Then we had some comedy. After I had waited a good two minutes there was a knock on the door and O'Hara called come in. The door swung wide open and two individuals entered with guns in their hands, stern and alert. When they saw the arrangements they stopped dead and looked foolish.

"What do you want?" O'Hara barked.

"The phone," one said. "Goodwin. We didn't know . . ."

"For Christ's sake!" Purley exploded. "Ain't I here?" It was a breach of discipline, with his superiors present.

They bumped at the threshold, getting out, pulling the door after them. I couldn't possibly have been blamed for helping myself to another hearty laugh, but there's a limit to what even a Deputy Commissioner will take, so I choked it off and sat tight until there was a voice in my ear that I knew better than any other voice on earth.

"Archie," I said.

"Where are you?" The voice was icy with rage, but not at me.

"I'm in O'Hara's office, at his desk, using his phone. I am half starved. O'Hara, Cramer, and Sergeant Stebbins are present. To be perfectly fair, Cramer and Purley are innocent. This boneheaded play was a solo by O'Hara. He fully realizes his mistake and sincerely apologizes. The warrant for my arrest is a thing of the past. The letter about Miss Vance is in my pocket. I have conceded nothing. I'm free to go where I please, including home. O'Hara requests, as a personal favor, that you kill the announcement you gave WPIT. Can that be done?"

"It can if I choose. It was arranged through Mr. Richards."

"So I suspected. You should have seen O'Hara's face when the tidings reached him. If you choose, and all of us here hope you do, go ahead and kill it and I'll be there in twenty minutes or less. Tell Fritz I'm hungry."

"Mr. O'Hara is a nincompoop. Tell him I said so. I'll have the announcement suspended temporarily, but there will be conditions. Stay there. I'll phone you shortly."

I cradled the phone, leaned back, and grinned at the three inquiring faces. "He'll call back. He thinks he can head it off temporarily, but he's got some idea about conditions."

I focused on O'Hara. "He said to tell you that he says you're a nincompoop, but I think it would be more tactful not to mention it, so I won't."

"Someday," O'Hara said, "he'll land on his nose."

They all sat down and began exchanging comments. I didn't listen because my mind was occupied. I was willing to chalk up for Wolfe a neat and well-timed swagger, and to admit that it got the desired results, but now what? Did he really have anything at all, and if so how much? It had better be fairly good. Cramer and Stebbins were not exactly ready to clasp our hands across the corpses, and as for O'Hara, I only hoped to God that when Wolfe called back he wouldn't tell me to slap the Deputy Commissioner on the back and tell him it had been just a prank and wasn't it fun? All in all, it was such a gloomy outlook that when the buzzer sounded and I reached for the phone I would just as soon have been somewhere else.

Wolfe's voice asked if they were still there and I said yes. He said to tell them that the announcement had been postponed and would not be broadcast at ten o'clock, and I did so. Then he asked for my report of the day's events.

"Now?" I demanded. "On the phone?"

"Yes," he said. "Concisely, but including all essentials. If there is a contradiction to demolish I must know it."

Even with the suspicion gnawing at me that I had got roped in for a supporting role in an enormous bluff, I did enjoy it. It was a situation anyone would appreciate. There I was, in O'Hara's chair at his desk in his office, giving a detailed report to Wolfe of a murder I had witnessed and a police operation I had helped with, and for over half an hour those three bozos simply utterly had to sit and listen. Whatever position they might be in all too soon, all they could do now was to take it and like it. I did enjoy it. Now and then Wolfe interrupted with a question, and when I had finished he took me back to fill in a few gaps. Then he proceeded to give me instructions, and as I listened it became apparent that if it was a bluff at least he wasn't going to leave me behind the enemy lines to fight my way out. I asked him to repeat it to make sure I had it straight. He did so.

"Okay," I said. "Tell Fritz I'm hungry." I hung up and faced the three on chairs:

"I'm sorry it took so long, but he pays my salary and what could I do? As I told you, the announcement has been postponed. He is willing to kill it, but that sort of depends.

He thinks it would be appropriate for Inspector Cramer and Sergeant Stebbins to help with the windup. He would appreciate it if you will start by delivering eight people at his office as soon as possible. He wants the five who were at the Fraser apartment today, not including the girl, Nancylee, or Cora the cook. Also Savarese. Also Anderson, president of the Hi-Spot Company, and Owen, the public relations man. All he wants you to do is to get them there, and to be present yourselves, but with the understanding that he will run the show. With that provision, he states that when you leave you will be prepared to make an arrest and take the murderer with you, and the announcement he gave WPIT will not be made. You can do the announcing."

I arose and moved, crossing to a chair over by the wall near the door to reclaim my hat and coat. Then I turned:

"It's after ten o'clock, and if this thing is on I'm not going to start it on an empty stomach. In my opinion, even if all he has in mind is a game of blind man's bluff, which I doubt, it's well worth it. Orchard died twenty-five days ago. Beula Poole nine days. Miss Koppel ten hours. You could put your inventory on a postage stamp." I had my hand on the doorknob. "How about it? Feel like helping?"

Cramer growled at me, "Why Anderson and Owen? What does he want them for?"

"Search me. Of course he likes a good audience."

"Maybe we can't get them."

"You can try. You're an inspector and murder is a very bad crime."

"It may take hours."

"Yeah, it looks like an all-night party. If I can stand it you can, not to mention Mr. Wolfe. All right, then we'll be seeing you." I opened the door and took a step, but turned:

"Oh, I forgot, he told me to tell you, this anonymous letter about Elinor Vance is just some homemade bait that didn't get used. I typed it myself this morning. If you get a chance tonight you can do a sample on my machine and compare."

O'Hara barked ferociously, "Why the hell didn't you say so?"

"I didn't like the way I was asked, Commissioner. The only man I know of more sensitive than me is Nero Wolfe."

24

IT WAS not surprising that Cramer delivered the whole order. Certainly none of those people could have been compelled to go out into the night, and let themselves be conveyed to Nero Wolfe's office, or any place else, without slapping a charge on them, but it doesn't take much compelling when you're in that kind of a fix. They were all there well before midnight.

Wolfe stayed up in his room until they all arrived. I had supposed that while I ate my warmed-over cutlets he would have some questions or instructions for me, and probably both, but no. If he had anything he already had it and needed no contributions from me. He saw to it that my food was hot and my salad crisp and then beat it upstairs.

The atmosphere, as they gathered, was naturally not very genial, but it wasn't so much tense as it was glum. They were simply sunk. As soon as Elinor Vance got onto a chair she rested her elbows on her knees and buried her face in her hands, and stayed that way. Tully Strong folded his arms, let his head sag until his chin met his chest, and shut his eyes. Madeline Fraser sat in the red leather chair, which I got her into before President Anderson arrived, looking first at one of her fellow beings and then at another, but she gave the impression that she merely felt she ought to be conscious of something and they would do as well as anything else.

Bill Meadows, seated near Elinor Vance, was leaning back with his hands clasped behind his head, glaring at the ceiling. Nat Traub was a sight, with his necktie off center, his hair mussed, and his eyes bloodshot. His facial growth was the kind that needs shaving twice a day, and it hadn't had it. He was so restless he couldn't stay in his chair, but when he left it there was no place he wanted to go, so all he could do was sit down again. I did not, on that account, tag him for it, since he had a right to be haggard. A Meltette taken from a box delivered by him had poisoned and killed someone, and it wasn't hard to imagine how his client had reacted to that.

Two conversations were going on. Professor Savarese was telling Purley Stebbins something at length, presumably the latest in formulas, and Purley was making himself an accessory by nodding now and then. Anderson and Owen, the Hi-Spot delegates, were standing by the couch talking with Cramer, and, judging from the snatches I caught, they might finally decide to sit down and they might not. They had been the last to arrive. I, having passed the word to Wolfe that the delivery had been completed, was wondering what was keeping him when I heard the sound of his elevator.

They were so busy with their internal affairs that Traub and I were the only ones who were aware that our host had joined us until he reached the corner of his desk and turned to make a survey. The conversations stopped. Savarese bounded across to shake hands. Elinor Vance lifted her head, showing such a woebegone face that I had to restrain an impulse to take the anonymous letter from my pocket and tear it up then and there. Traub sat down for the twentieth time. Bill Meadows unclasped his hands and pressed his finger tips against his eyes. President Anderson sputtered:

"Since when have you been running the Police Department?"

That's what a big executive is supposed to do, go straight to the point.

Wolfe, getting loose from Savarese, moved to his chair and got himself arranged in it. I guess it's partly his size, unquestionably impressive, which holds people's attention when he is in motion, but his manner and style have a lot to do with it. You get both suspense and surprise. You know he's going to be clumsy and wait to see it, but by gum you never do. First thing you know there he is, in his chair or wherever he was bound for, and there was nothing clumsy about it at all. It was smooth and balanced and efficient.

He looked up at the clock, which said twenty to twelve, and remarked to the audience, "It's late, isn't it?" He regarded the Hi-Spot president:

"Let's not start bickering, Mr. Anderson. You weren't dragged here by force, were you? You were impelled either by concern or curiosity. In either case you won't leave until you hear what I have to say, so why not sit down and listen? If you want to be contentious wait until you learn what you have to contend with. It works better that way."

He took in the others. "Perhaps, though, I should answer Mr. Anderson's question, though it was obviously rhe-

141

torical. I am not running the Police Department, far from it. I don't know what you were told when you were asked to come here, but I assume you know that nothing I say is backed by any official authority, for I have none. Mr. Cramer and Mr. Stebbins are present as observers. That is correct, Mr. Cramer?"

The Inspector, seated on the corner of the couch, nodded. "They understand that."

"Good. Then Mr. Anderson's question was not only rhetorical, it was gibberish. I shall—"

"I have a question!" a voice said, harsh and strained.

"Yes, Mr. Meadows, what is it?"

"If this isn't official, what happens to the notes Goodwin is making?"

"That depends on what we accomplish. They may never leave this house, and end up by being added to the stack in the cellar. Or a transcription of them may be accepted as evidence in a courtroom.—I wish you'd sit down, Mr. Savarese. It's more tranquil if everyone is seated."

Wolfe shifted his center of gravity. During his first ten minutes in a chair minor adjustments were always required.

"I should begin," he said with just a trace of peevishness, "by admitting that I am in a highly vulnerable position. I have told Mr. Cramer that when he leaves here he will take a murderer with him; but though I know who the murderer is, I haven't a morsel of evidence against him, and neither has anyone else. Still—"

"Wait a minute," Cramer growled.

Wolfe shook his head. "It's important, Mr. Cramer, to keep this unofficial -until I reach a certain point, if I ever do—so it would be best for you to say nothing whatever." His eyes moved. "I think the best approach is to explain how I learned the identity of the murderer -and by the way, here's an interesting point: though I was already close to certitude, it was clinched for me only two hours ago, when Mr. Goodwin told me that there were sixteen eager candidates for the sponsorship just abandoned by Hi-Spot. That removed my shred of doubt."

"For God's sake," Nat Traub blurted, "let the fine points go! Let's have it!"

"You'll have to be patient, sir," Wolfe reproved him. "I'm not merely reporting, I'm doing a job. Whether a murderer gets arrested, and tried, and convicted, depends entirely on how I handle this. There is no evidence, and if I don't squeeze it out of you people now, tonight, there may never be any. The trouble all along, both for the police and for me, has been that no finger pointed without wavering. In going for a murderer as well concealed as this one it is always necessary to trample down improbabilities to get a path started, but it is foolhardy to do so until a direction is plainly indicated. This time there was no such plain indication, and, frankly, I had begun to doubt if there would be one—until yesterday morning, when Mr. Anderson and Mr. Owen visited this office. They gave it to me."

"You're a liar!" Anderson stated.

"You see?" Wolfe upturned a palm. "Some day, sir, you're going to get on the wrong train by trying to board yours before it arrives. How do you know whether I'm a liar or not until you know what I'm saying? You did come here. You gave me a check for the full amount of my fee, told me that I was no longer in your hire, and said that you had withdrawn as a sponsor of Miss Fraser's program. You gave as your reason for withdrawal that the practice of blackmail had been injected into the case, and you didn't want your product connected in the public mind with blackmail because it is dirty and makes people gag. Isn't that so?"

"Yes. But—"

"I'll do the butting. After you left I sat in this chair twelve straight hours, with intermissions only for meals, using my brain on you. If I had known then that before the day was out sixteen other products were scrambling to take your Hi-Spot's place, I would have reached my conclusion in much less than twelve hours, but I didn't. What I was exploring was the question, what had happened to you? You had been so greedy for publicity that you had even made a trip down here to get into a photograph with me. Now, suddenly, you were fleeing like a comely maiden from a smallpox scare. Why?"

"I told you—"

"I know. But that wasn't good enough. Examined with care, it was actually flimsy. I don't propose to recite all my twistings and windings for those twelve hours, but first of all I rejected the reason you gave. What, then? I considered every possible circumstance and all conceivable combinations. That you were yourself the murderer and feared I might sniff you out; that you were not the murderer, but the blackmailer; that, yourself innocent, you knew the identity of one of the culprits, or both, and did not wish to be associated with the disclosure; and a thousand others. Upon each and all of my conjectures I brought to bear what I knew of you—your position, your record, your temperament, and your character. At the end only one supposition wholly satisfied me. I concluded that you had somehow become convinced that someone closely connected with that program, which you were sponsoring, had committed the murders, and that there was a possibility that that fact would be discovered. More: I concluded that it was not Miss Koppel or Miss Vance or Mr. Meadows or Mr. Strong, and certainly not Mr. Savarese. It is the public mind that you are anxious about, and in the public mind those people are quite insignificant. Miss Fraser is that program, and that program is Miss Fraser. It could only be her. You knew, or thought you knew, that Miss Fraser herself had killed Mr. Orchard, and possibly Miss Poole too, and you were getting as far away from her as you could as quickly as you could. Your face tells me you don't like that."

"No," Anderson said coldly, "and you won't either before you hear the last of it. You through?"

"Good heavens, no. I've barely started. As I say, I reached that conclusion, but it was nothing to crow about. What was I to do with it? I had a screw I could put on you, but it seemed unwise to be hasty about it, and I considered a trial of other expedients. I confess that the one I chose to begin with was feeble and even sleazy, but it was at breakfast this morning, before I had finished my coffee and got dressed, and Mr. Goodwin was fidgety and I wanted to give him something to do. Also, I had already made a suggestion to Mr. Cramer which was designed to give everyone the impression that there was evidence that Miss Vance had been blackmailed, that she was under acute suspicion, and that she might be charged with murder at any moment. There was a chance, I thought, that an imminent threat to Miss Vance, who is a personable young woman, might impel somebody to talk."

"So you started that," Elinor Vance said dully.

Wolfe nodded. "I'm not boasting about it. I've confessed it was worse than second-rate, but I thought Mr. Cramer might as well try it; and this morning, before I was dressed, I could devise nothing better than for Mr. Goodwin to type an anonymous letter about you and take it up there —a letter which implied that you had committed murder at least twice."

"Goddam pretty," Bill Meadows said.

"He didn't do it," Elinor said.

"Yes, he did," Wolfe disillusioned her. "He had it with him, but didn't get to use it. The death of Miss Koppel was responsible not only for that, but for other things as well —for instance, for this gathering. If I had acted swiftly and energetically on the conclusion I reached twenty-four hours ago, Miss Koppel might be alive now. I owe her an apology but I can't get it to her. What I can do is what I'm doing."

Wolfe's eyes darted to Anderson and fastened there. "I'm going to put that screw on you, sir. I won't waste time appealing to you, in the name of justice or anything else, to tell me why you abruptly turned tail and scuttled. That would be futile. Instead, I'll tell you a homely little fact: Miss Fraser drank Hi-Spot only the first few times it was served on her program, and then had to quit and substitute coffee. She had to quit because your product upset her stomach. It gave her a violent indigestion."

"That's a lie," Anderson said. "Another lie."

"If it is it won't last long. —Miss Vance. Some things aren't as important as they once were. You heard what I said. Is it true?"

"Yes."

"Mr. Strong?"

"I don't think this—"

"Confound it, you're in the same room and the same chair! Is it true or not?"

"Yes."

"Mr. Meadows?"

"Yes."

"That should be enough. —So, Mr. Anderson—"

"A put-up job," the president sneered. "I left their damn program."

Wolfe shook his head. "They're not missing you. They had their choice of sixteen offers. No, Mr. Anderson, you're in a pickle. Blackmail revolts you, and you're being blackmailed. It is true that newspapers are reluctant to offend advertisers, but some of them couldn't possibly resist so picturesque an item as this, that the product Miss Fraser puffed so effectively to ten million people made her so ill that she didn't dare swallow a spoonful of it. Indeed yes, the papers will print it; and they'll get it in time for Monday morning."

"You sonofabitch." Anderson was holding. "They won't touch it. Will they, Fred?"

145

But the director of public relations was frozen, speechless with horror.

"I think they will," Wolfe persisted. "One will, I know. And open publication might be better than the sort of talk that would get around when once it's started. You know how rumors get distorted; fools would even say that it wasn't necessary to add anything to Hi-Spot to poison Mr. Orchard. Really, the blackmail potential of this is very high. And what do you have to do to stop it? Something hideous and insupportable? Not at all. Merely tell me why you suddenly decided to scoot."

Anderson looked at Owen, but Owen was gazing fixedly at Wolfe as at the embodiment of evil.

"It will be useless," Wolfe said, "to try any dodge. I'm ready for you. I spent all day yesterday on this, and I doubt very much if I'll accept anything except what I have already specified: that someone or something had persuaded you that Miss Fraser herself was in danger of being exposed as a murderer or a blackmailer. However, you can try."

"I don't have to try." He was a stubborn devil. "I told you yesterday. That was my reason then, and it's my reason now."

"Oh, for God's sake!" Fred Owen wailed. "Oh, my God!"

"Goddam it," Anderson blurted at him. "I gave my word! I'm sewed up! I promised!"

"To whom?" Wolfe snapped.

"All right," Owen said bitterly, "keep your word and lose your shirt. This is ruin! This is dynamite!"

"To whom?" Wolfe persisted.

"I can't tell you, and I won't. That was part of the promise."

"Indeed. Then that makes it simple." Wolfe's eyes darted left. "Mr. Meadows, a hypothetical question. If it was you to whom Mr. Anderson gave the pledge that keeps him from speaking, do you now release him from it?"

"It wasn't me," Bill said.

"I didn't ask you that. You know what a hypothetical question is. Please answer to the if. If it was you, do you release him?"

"Yes. I do."

"Mr. Traub, the same question. With that if, do you release him?"

"Yes."

"Miss Vance? Do you?"

"Yes."

"Mr. Strong. Do you?"

Of course Tully Strong had had time, a full minute, to make up his mind what to say. He said it:

"No!"

25

ELEVEN pairs of eyes fastened on Tully Strong.

"Aha," Wolfe muttered. He leaned back, sighed deep, and looked pleased.

"Remarkable!" a voice boomed. It was Professor Savarese. "So simple!"

If he expected to pull some of the eyes his way, he got cheated. They stayed on Strong.

"That was a piece of luck," Wolfe said, "and I'm grateful for it. If I had started with you, Mr. Strong, and got your no, the others might have made it not so simple."

"I answered a hypothetical question," Tully asserted, "and that's all. It doesn't mean anything."

"Correct," Wolfe agreed. "In logic, it doesn't. But I saw your face when you realized what was coming, the dilemma you would be confronted with in a matter of seconds, and that was enough. Do you now hope to retreat into logic?"

Tully just wasn't up to it. Not only had his face been enough when he saw it coming; it was still enough. The muscles around his thin tight lips quivered as he issued the command to let words through.

"I merely answered a hypothetical question," was the best he could do. It was pathetic.

Wolfe sighed again. "Well. I suppose I'll have to light it for you. I don't blame you, sir, for being obstinate about it, since it may be assumed that you have behaved badly. I don't mean your withholding information from the police; most people do that, and often for reasons much shoddier than yours. I mean your behavior to your employers. Since you are paid by the eight sponsors jointly your loyalty to them is indivisible; but you did not warn all of them that Miss Fraser was, or might be, headed for disgrace and disaster, and that therefore they had better clear out; appar-

147

ently you confined it to Mr. Anderson. For value received or to be received, I presume—a good job?"

Wolfe shrugged. "But now it's all up." His eyes moved. "By the way, Archie, since Mr. Strong will soon be telling us how he knew it was Miss Fraser, you'd better take a look. She's capable of anything, and she's as deft as a bear's tongue. Look in her bag."

Cramer was on his feet. "I'm not going—"

"I didn't ask you," Wolfe snapped. "Confound it, don't you see how ticklish this is? I'm quite aware I've got no evidence yet, but I'm not going to have that woman displaying her extraordinary dexterity in my office. Archie?"

I had left my chair and stepped to the other end of Wolfe's desk, but I was in a rather embarrassing position. I am not incapable of using force on a woman, since after all men have never found anything else to use on them with any great success when it comes right down to it, but Wolfe had by no means worked up to a point where the audience was with me. And when I extended a hand toward the handsome leather bag in Madeline Fraser's lap, she gave me the full force of her gray-green eyes and told me distinctly:

"Don't touch me."

I brought the hand back. Her eyes went to Wolfe.

"Don't you think it's about time I said something? Wouldn't it look better?"

"No." Wolfe met her gaze. "I'd advise you to wait, madam. All you can give us now is a denial, and of course we'll stipulate that. What else can you say?"

"I wouldn't bother with a denial," she said scornfully. "But it seems stupid for me to sit here and let this go on indefinitely."

"Not at all." Wolfe leaned toward her. "Let me assure you of one thing, Miss Fraser, most earnestly. It is highly unlikely, whatever you say or do from now on, that I shall ever think you stupid. I am too well convinced of the contrary. Not even if Mr. Goodwin opens your bag and finds in it the gun with which Miss Poole was shot."

"He isn't going to open it."

She seemed to know what she was talking about. I glanced at Inspector Cramer, but the big stiff wasn't ready yet to move a finger. I picked up the little table that was always there by the arm of the red leather chair, moved it over to the wall, went and brought one of the small yellow chairs, and sat, so close to Madeline Fraser that if we had spread elbows they would have touched. That meant no more notes, but Wolfe couldn't have everything. As I sat down by her, putting in motion the air that had been there undisturbed, I got a faint whiff of a spicy perfume, and my imagination must have been pretty active because I was reminded of the odor that had reached me that day in her apartment, from the breath of Deborah Koppel as I tried to get her onto the divan before she collapsed. It wasn't the same at all except in my fancy. I asked Wolfe:

"This will do, won't it?"

He nodded and went back to Tully Strong. "So you have not one reason for reluctance, but several. Even so, you can't possibly stick it. It has been clearly demonstrated to Mr. Cramer that you are withholding important information directly pertinent to the crimes he is investigating, and you and others have already pushed his patience pretty far. He'll get his teeth in you now and he won't let go. Then there's Mr. Anderson. The promise he gave you is half gone, now that we know it was you he gave it to, and with the threat I'm holding over him he can't reasonably be expected to keep the other half."

Wolfe gestured. "And all I really need is a detail. I am satisfied that I know pretty well what you told Mr. Anderson. What happened yesterday, just before he took alarm and leaped to action? The morning papers had the story of the anonymous letters—the blackmailing device by which people were constrained to make payments to Mr. Orchard and Miss Poole. Then that story had supplied a missing link for someone. Who and how? Say it was Mr. Anderson. Say that he received, some weeks ago, an anonymous letter or letters blackguarding Miss Fraser. He showed them to her. He received no more letters. That's all he knew about it. A little later Mr. Orchard was a guest on the Fraser program and got poisoned, but there was no reason for Mr. Anderson to connect that event with the anonymous letters he had received. That was what the story in yesterday's papers did for him; they made that connection. It was now perfectly plain: anonymous letters about Miss Fraser; Miss Fraser's subscription to *Track Almanac;* the method by which those subscriptions were obtained; and Mr. Orchard's death by drinking poisoned coffee ostensibly intended for Miss Fraser. That did not convict Miss Fraser of murder, but at a minimum it made it extremely inadvisable to continue in the role of her sponsor. So Mr. Anderson skedaddled."

"I got no anonymous letters," Anderson declared.

"I believe you." Wolfe didn't look away from Tully Strong. "I rejected, tentatively, the assumption that Mr. Anderson had himself received the anonymous letters, on various grounds, but chiefly because it would be out of character for him to show an anonymous letter to the subject of it. He would be much more likely to have the letter's allegations investigated, and there was good reason to assume that that had not been done. So I postulated that it was not Mr. Anderson, but some other person, who had once received an anonymous letter or letters about Miss Fraser and who was yesterday provided with a missing link. It was a permissible guess that that person was one of those now present, and so I tried the experiment of having the police insinuate an imminent threat to Miss Vance, in the hope that it would loosen a tongue. I was too cautious. It failed lamentably; and Miss Koppel died."

Wolfe was talking only to Strong. "Of course, having no evidence, I have no certainty that the information you gave Mr. Anderson concerned anonymous letters. It is possible that your conviction, or suspicion, about Miss Fraser, had some other basis. But I like my assumption because it is neat and comprehensive; and I shall abandon it only under compulsion. It explains everything, and nothing contradicts it. It will even explain, I confidently expect, why Mr. Orchard and Miss Poole were killed. Two of the finer points of their operation were these, that they demanded only a small fraction of the victims income, limited to one year, and that the letters did not expose, or threaten to expose, an actual secret in the victim's past. Even if they had known such secrets they would not have used them. But sooner or later —this is a point on which Mr. Savarese could speak with the authority of an expert, but not now, some other time—sooner or later, by the law of averages, they would use such a secret by inadvertence. Sooner or later the bugaboo they invented would be, for the victim, not a mischievous libel, but a real and most dreadful terror."

Wolfe nodded. "Yes. So it happened. The victim was shown the letter or letters by some friend—by you, Mr. Strong—and found herself confronted not merely by the necessity of paying an inconsequential tribute, but by the awful danger of some disclosure that was not to be borne; for she could not know, of course, that the content of the letter had been fabricated and that its agreement with reality was sheer accident. So she acted. Indeed, she acted! She killed Mr. Orchard. Then she learned, from a strange female voice on the phone, that Mr. Orchard had not been the sole possessor of the knowledge she thought he had, and again she acted. She killed Miss Poole."

"My God," Anderson cut in, "you're certainly playing it strong, with no cards."

"I am, sir," Wolfe agreed. "It's time I got dealt to, don't you think? Surely I've earned at least one card. You can give it to me, or Mr. Strong can. What more do you want, for heaven's sake? Rabbits from a hat?"

Anderson got up, moved, and was confronting the secretary of the Sponsors' Council. "Don't be a damn fool, Tully," he said with harsh authority. "He knows it all, you heard him. Go ahead and get rid of it!"

"This is swell for me," Tully said bitterly.

"It would have been swell for Miss Koppel," Wolfe said curtly, "if you had spoken twenty hours ago. How many letters did you get?"

"Two."

"When?"

"February. Around the middle of February."

"Did you show them to anyone besides Miss Fraser?"

"No, just her, but Miss Koppel was there so she saw them too."

"Where are they now?"

"I don't know. I gave them to Miss Fraser."

"What did they say?"

Tully's lips parted, stayed open a moment, and closed again.

"Don't be an ass," Wolfe snapped. "Mr. Anderson is here. What did they say?"

"They said that it was lucky for Miss Fraser that when her husband died no one had been suspicious enough to have the farewell letters he wrote examined by a hand-writing expert."

"What else?"

"That was all. The second one said the same thing, only in a different way."

Wolfe's eyes darted to Anderson. "Is that what he told you, sir?"

The president, who had returned to the couch, nodded. "Yes, that's it. Isn't it enough?"

"Plenty, in the context." Wolfe's head jerked around to face the lady at my elbow. "Miss Fraser. I've heard of only one farewell letter your husband wrote, to a friend, a local attorney. Was there another? To you, perhaps?"

"I don't think," she said, "that it would be very sensible for me to try to help you." I couldn't detect the slightest difference in her voice. Wolfe had understated it when he said she was an extremely dangerous woman. "Especially," she went on, "since you are apparently accepting those lies. If Mr. Strong ever got any anonymous letters he never showed them to me—nor to Miss Koppel, I'm sure of that."

"I'll be damned!" Tully Strong cried, and his specs fell off as he gawked at her.

It was marvelous, and it certainly showed how Madeline Fraser got people. Tully had been capable of assuming that she had killed a couple of guys, but when he heard her come out with what he knew to be a downright lie he was flabbergasted.

Wolfe nodded at her. "I suppose," he admitted, "it would be hopeless to expect you to be anything but sensible. You are aware that there is still no evidence, except Mr. Strong's word against yours. Obviously the best chance is the letter your husband wrote to his friend, since the threat that aroused your ferocity concerned it." His face left us, to the right. "Do you happen to know, Mr. Cramer, whether that letter still exists?"

Cramer was right up with him. He had gone to the phone on my desk and was dialing. In a moment he spoke:

"Dixon there? Put him on. Dixon? I'm at Wolfe's office. Yeah, he's got it, but by the end of the tail. Two things quick. Get Darst and have him phone Fleetville, Michigan. He was out there and knows 'em. Before Lawrence Koppel died he wrote a letter to a friend. We want to know if that letter still exists and where it is, and they're to get it if they can and keep it, but for God's sake don't scare the friend into burning it or eating it. Tell Darst it's so important it's the whole case. Then get set with a warrant for an all-day job on the Fraser woman's apartment. What we're looking for is cyanide, and it can be anywhere—the heel of a shoe, for instance. You know the men to get—only the best. Wolfe got it by the tail with one of his crazy dives into a two-foot tank, and now we've got to hang onto it. What? Yes, damn it, of course it's her! Step on it!"

He hung up, crossed to me, thumbed me away, moved the chair aside, and stood by Miss Fraser's chair, gazing down at her. Keeping his gaze where it was, he rumbled:

"You might talk a little more, Wolfe."

"I could talk all night," Wolfe declared. "Miss Fraser is

worth it. She had good luck, but most of the bad luck goes to the fumblers, and she is no fumbler. Her husband's death must have been managed with great skill, not so much because she gulled the authorities, which may have been no great feat, but because she completely deceived her husband's sister, Miss Koppel. The whole operation with Mr. Orchard was well conceived and executed, with the finest subtlety in even the lesser details—for instance, having the subscription in Miss Koppel's name. It was simple to phone Mr. Orchard that that money came from her, Miss Fraser. But best of all was the climax—getting the poisoned coffee served to the intended victim. That was one of her pieces of luck, since apparently Mr. Traub, who didn't know about the taped bottle, innocently put it in front of Mr. Orchard, but she would have managed without it. At that narrow table, with Mr. Orchard just across from her, and with the broadcast going on, she could have manipulated it with no difficulty, and probably without anyone becoming aware of any manipulation. Certainly without arousing any suspicion of intent, before or after."

"Okay," Cramer conceded. "That doesn't worry me. And the Poole thing doesn't either, since there's nothing against it. But the Koppel woman?"

Wolfe nodded. "That was the masterpiece. Miss Fraser had in her favor, certainly, years of intimacy during which she had gained Miss Koppel's unquestioning loyalty, affection, and trust. They held steadfast even when Miss Koppel saw the anonymous letters Mr. Strong had received. It is quite possible that she received similar letters herself. We don't know, and never will, I suppose, what finally gave birth to the worm of suspicion in Miss Koppel. It wasn't the newspaper story of the anonymous letters and blackmailing, since that appeared yesterday, Friday, and it was on Wednesday that Miss Koppel tried to take an airplane to Michigan. We may now assume, since we know that she had seen the anonymous letters, that something had made her suspicious enough to want to inspect the farewell letter her brother had sent to his friend, and we may certainly assume that Miss Fraser, when she learned what her dearest and closest friend had tried to do, knew why."

"That's plain enough," Cramer said impatiently. "What I mean—"

"I know. You mean what I meant when I said it was a masterpiece. It took resourcefulness, first-rate improvisation, and ingenuity to make use of the opportunity offered by Mr. Traub's delivery of the box of Meltettes; and only a maniacal stoicism could have left those deadly tidbits there on the piano where anybody might casually have eaten one. Probably inquiry would show that it was not as haphazard as it seems; that it was generally known that the box was there to be sampled by Miss Fraser and therefore no one would loot it. But the actual performance, as Mr. Goodwin described it to me, was faultless. There was then no danger to a bystander, for if anyone but Miss Koppel had started to eat one of the things Miss Fraser could easily have prevented it. If the box had been handed to Miss Fraser, she could either have postponed the sampling or have taken one from the second layer instead of the top. What chance was there that Miss Koppel would eat one of the things? One in five, one in a thousand? Anyway, she played for that chance, and again she had luck; but it was not all luck, and she performed superbly."

"This is incredible," Madeline Fraser said. "I knew I was strong, but I didn't know I could do this. Only a few hours ago my dearest friend Debby died in my arms. I should be with her, sitting with her through the night, but here I am, sitting here, listening to this . . . this nightmare . . ."

"Cut," Bill Meadows said harshly. "Night and nightmare. Cut one."

The gray-green eyes darted at him. "So you're ratting, are you, Bill?"

"Yes, I'm ratting. I saw Debby die. And I think he's got it. I think you killed her."

"Bill!" It was Elinor Vance, breaking. "Bill, I can't stand it!" She was on her feet, shaking all over. "I can't!"

Bill put his arms around her, tight. "All right, kid. I hope to God she gets it. You were there too. What if you had decided to eat one?"

The phone rang and I got it. It was for Cramer. Purley went and replaced him beside Miss Fraser, and he came to the phone. When he hung up he told Wolfe:

"Koppel's friend still has that letter, and it's safe."

"Good," Wolfe said approvingly. "Will you please get her out of here? I've been wanting beer for an hour, and I'm not foolhardy enough to eat or drink anything with her in the house." He looked around. "The rest of you are invited to stay if you care to. You must be thirsty."

But they didn't like it there. They went.

154

26

THE EXPERTS were enthusiastic about the letter Lawrence Koppel had written to his friend. They called it one of the cleverest forgeries they had ever seen. But what pleased Wolfe most was the finding of the cyanide. It was in the hollowed-out heel of a house slipper, and was evidently the leavings of the supply Mrs. Lawrence Koppel had snitched six years ago from her husband's shelf.

It was May eighteenth that she was sentenced on her conviction for the first-degree murder of Deborah Koppel. They had decided that was the best one to try her for. The next day, a Wednesday, a little before noon, Wolfe and I were in the office checking over catalogues when the phone rang. I went to my desk for it.

"Nero Wolfe's office, Archie Goodwin speaking."

"May I speak to Mr. Wolfe, please?"

"Who is it?"

"Tell him a personal matter."

I covered the transmitter. "Personal matter," I told Wolfe. "A man whose name I have forgotten."

"What the devil! Ask him."

"A man," I said distinctly, "whose name I have forgotten."

"Oh." He frowned. He finished checking an item and then picked up the phone on his desk, while I stayed with mine. "This is Nero Wolfe."

"I would know the voice anywhere. How are you?"

"Well, thank you. Do I know you?"

"Yes. I am calling to express my appreciation of your handling of the Fraser case, now that it's over. I am pleased and thought you should know it. I have been, and still am, a little annoyed, but I am satisfied that you are not responsible. I have good sources of information. I congratulate you on keeping your investigation within the limits I prescribed. That has increased my admiration of you."

"I like to be admired," Wolfe said curtly. "But when I undertake an investigation I permit prescription of limits only by the requirements of the job. If that job had taken me across your path you would have found me there."

"Then that is either my good fortune—or yours."

The connection went.

I grinned at Wolfe. "He's an abrupt bastard."

Wolfe grunted. I returned to my post at the end of his desk and picked up my pencil.

"One little idea," I suggested. "Why not give Dr. Michaels a ring and ask if anyone has phoned to switch his subscription? No, that won't do, he's paid up. Marie Leconne?"

"No. I invite trouble only when I'm paid for it. And to grapple with him the pay would have to be high."

"Okay." I checked an item. "You'd be a problem in a fox-hole, but the day may come."

"It may. I hope not. Have you any Zygopetalum crinitum on that page?"

"Good God no. It begins with a Z!"